Great Snoring, Norfolk

The British Isles are awash with tales concerning the apparitions of ghostly black hounds that terrify the unsuspecting traveller, none more so than in Norfolk.

One in particular, in this case, "The White Shuck of Great Snoring," caught my interest – not surprising as it's the village where my father was born and raised. Said to be a harbinger of doom, it was sighted several times on the eve of The Second World War, slinking along the lonely roads between the villages. It would dash in front of cyclists and wayfarers and disappear into the fields, and, on one occasion, left a motorist so unnerved, he abandoned his vehicle.

Old Shuggy

"It's not far now, you can see the outline of the church through the murk."

A delicate hand emerged from the sleeve of her duffle coat, and she took him by the arm.

The fog sank onto them like smoke, except it felt cold and wet against his face. His throat itched and his nose was numb with the chill. Everywhere was still and silent. Curlews warbled sulkily from somewhere out there on the sand – an open expanse shrouded by the rolling sea mist.

Ooom … Ooom

The muffled thuds of the bitterns' calls sounded ominous, reminding him of distant gunfire … or human cries of anguish. A plop of water from over the hidden mud flats and reeds broke the uneasy quietude. The curlews were feeding. In his mind's eye, he saw a bloodworm slip down the beak and into the gullet of the beady-eyed creature. He shivered.

"We should stick to the paving stones," she said. "In this poor visibility, you don't know where the shingle gives way to the tidal marshes and creeks."

She must have noticed his grimace because she tugged at his sleeve encouragingly and quickened her pace, her small, wiry frame puffing misty breath as she steered them on.

The church stood on a sloping spit of land that jutted out onto the shoreline; a not altogether untypical occurrence along this stretch of the Norfolk coastline, he reminded himself.

The mist was getting thicker. It moved and curled around them like tendrils; a living, creeping sentience stalking the silent air. Its greyness hung over the dunes and shingle and its dullness blended with the listless sky so that the horizon no longer existed. As they drew nearer the blackened silhouette of the church and steeple emerged like an encroaching leviathan.

"It's worth it you'll see," Izzy said, her voice shrill in the silent ether. She brushed aside a wispy locket of hair that tumbled from her woolly hat and danced across her eyes. Even her face seemed grey in this light.

"C'mon, we'll enter by the west door." She disappeared behind a buttress of the church wall, and he struggled to follow; there was no pathway or gate to guide him. The trail had long since vanished, or was choked and hidden amid the invading gorse and brambles, as were the crumbling and weathered gravestones. The door was unlocked, and after they had stepped inside, Izzy pushed hard against its heavy oak panels. It shut with a clank, and the resounding echo of the latch extinguished the breathing sigh of the sea beyond the walls. Funny, he hadn't noticed how the sea breathed before; its sudden snuffing out accentuated the stillness and silence.

He wandered down the nave of the church. The smell of damp and must almost made him hanker for the salty seaweed air and mist they had retreated from. He fingered idly through the tatty parish notices and leaflets littering a table and pondered at the row of bibles scattered on the polished worn pews. The whole place reeked of neglect and sadness.

Then, a click of a switch and the grimy whitewashed walls glowed a fluorescent blue. Izzy remained by the door. "Over there, on the opposite side, in an aisle beyond the rood screen of the altar… take a look."

Tucked away in an alcove hidden from the main body of the building, a display case lodged recumbent in a stone recess within the wall. He approached and peered inside. Embedded in what appeared to be dried clay were the skeletal remains of a headless, four legged beast, and incorporated into the glass casing, a heavily tarnished plaque read:

"Our very own Black Shuck

"Before you lies the remains of a black hound without a head found by workmen when digging on consecrated ground in the year of our Lord eighteen hundred and sixteen.

"Pay him a penny and he shall let you pass. Pay him nothing and face a portent of your doom."

"A good means I suppose to help with the church restoration fund." He sniffed the musty atmosphere and threw a cursory glance at the flaky dry rot of the rafters above. He fumbled for the small change in his pocket and searched for the nearby donation box. Then he thought better of it, and with a mixture of derision and defiance, he dropped the coins back into his pocket.

"No, why should I? It's probably the remains of a sheep or goat or some such." He sniffed again, but jumped, suddenly aware of Izzy's presence as she nudged him in his midriff.

And whether they belonged to the beast or not, someone had placed a pair of canine fangs the size of two inch nails beside the severed neck bone.

"I thought you'd be interested." She clung to his arm again. "Especially after your encounter with the ghostly dog on Snoring Road the other day."

"I wish I hadn't mentioned that."

"We should go," she said disappointedly, "before darkness sets in - the mudflats and marshes are dangerous and will claim us. You can tell Uncle Abram all about your encounter yesterday with Shuggy."

"No, he'll laugh."

"He won't, it's just his way that's all. You got on

well with him last night didn't you?"

"Only 'cos he beat me at chess four games in a row."

"No, tell him; he's very scholarly, you know, in spite of his manner."

They made for the door and he slammed it behind them hastily. The wet chill assaulted him and the huff of the invisible waves resounded … the slumbering breath of a giant shrouded in the haze.

Izzy cocked her ear. "The haar's rolling in from the sea. We should hasten."

The image of Shuck's dry bones lingered, and as they retreated, he stole a glance at the diminishing outline of the church. They had forgotten to extinguish the lights, and pale, yellow beams spilled from a pair of windows, penetrating the fog, and reminding him of smouldering amber coals akin to the waking eyes of the hound.

They found their way back to the dryer, sandier dunes and headed towards the hamlet.

"And you never looked at the war memorial. Uncle Abram's father and grandfather have their names inscribed – they died in The Great War."

The dull boom of the bitterns still thudded through the stillness like cannon on the distant horizon, adding poignancy to Izzy's remark.

***

Zing – hiss –

Another toenail clipping shot into the fire glowing in the grate.

"Bull's-eye!" Uncle Abram was triumphant and he positioned the clippers on the next toe.

"What's this abou' yooor' meeting with owl' Shuggy then, boye'?"

His bright and intelligent eye shifted momentarily from the clipper and the gnarled foot, and settled on him.

"Oh, the ghostly black dog. Izzy told you about that did she?"

"She tells me abou' everythin' does tha young mawther of mine."

Izzy's voice came from the kitchen, beyond the low doorway of the darkened room. "Listen to him, Uncle."

He hesitated before beginning his story and surveyed his surroundings. The glowing red hue of the coal embers scarcely penetrated the hidden recesses of the room, which were further obscured by the clutter of ancient and redundant furniture. This was the only part of the cottage occupied now; the bed, the dining table and bookshelves, all surrounded them. Abram, widowed, alone, his body failing him, saw little use for upstairs, and it was irrelevant to him, just as much as the airs of social convention.

Zing – another clipping shot through the air.

It was the perfect setting for a ghost story, so he might as well tell it to the old man. He put his faith in Izzy.

"Well it was yesterday afternoon. We – Izzy and I – were cycling along Snoring Lane, back from the pub in the main village. Izzy had forged ahead of me as always and had disappeared from sight. As I peddled away, the lane veered around a long bend and down a hill so the cycle began to gather speed. A dense spinney blanketed the landscape on my near side, but the afternoon sun blazed onto the hay meadows opposite."

Zing – any closer and it would have taken his eye out.

"I could could barely recognise the remains of the old corn mill as I approached; it was difficult as the crumbling brick walls were obscured by the undergrowth of dried grass and bracken. Then something caught my eye – an object appeared to dart from the ruins. A creature … a *thing,* had emerged into the sunlight and was blocking the road ahead of me. It was one of those moments when you frown to yourself as your brain tries to make sense of what's in front of you.

"It was nothing more than a featureless black blob. It seemed to absorb all the light around it, and … it moved, it *crept* … almost like a huge tarantula! Evil looking thing it was."

A sly smile formed on the old man's lips. Suddenly he felt stupid; he should have known. "But that's absurd, of course."

"Go on, you're doing well." Izzy called from the kitchen, egging him on.

"You concentrate on thur supper, young woman." Abram smiled at her affectionately. "She's a good 'un bu' jist like her mother, God res' her, she's anarl innocen' and has her hid' in thur clouds."

There was no going back now. "Well … I clamped on the handbrakes and the bike juddered to a halt. I don't mind telling you I had the jitters because the screeching noise from the cycle frame caused the 'tarantula' to halt. It was so still – inert, you could say – it wasn't natural. I couldn't make out its features in spite of the sunlight, and maybe it was my imagination, but I kept thinking that it was watching me …weighing me up.

"Then, after what seemed ages, the creature continued its swagger across the lane and it disappeared into the woods opposite.

"So I perched there, feet off the peddles and dangling, and hands gripping the handlebars thinking on what to do. I had to pass by the spot, there was no alternative. I peddled like fury down the hill, gathering speed and momentum so as to rise up the oncoming gradient in as shorter time as possible. I was sure that at any moment the beast would pounce.

"But it never did, and once I was out among the open fields again, my fear left me."

He trailed off, waiting for an onslaught of mockery from Uncle Abram, but instead he reached for his woolly sock and covered his gnarled foot.

He replied with a broad, tooth gapped smile. "No spider, bu' a dog. Yow are not thur firs' to hev seen 'owl Shuggy along tha' drift, bu' it's usuallie by thur' young fules ar'er spendin' toime in thur pub anarl much cider.

"I've spen' all moi life in those fields, haymakin' and gatherin' spuds until the screws in moi back go' so blomin' sore, Oi had to give it up, bu' in all tha toime Oi navver saw it. Noo Black Shuggy for me. Bu'moi father an' my grandfather and his brothers, thay all saw him. And where are thay now eh? All killed in wars. What's tha' say to yow eh? Yow see owl' Shuggy and it's a portent of doom. That's waa thay say."

Abram's reply surprised him, and when he peered through the dull, reddened gloom around him, the glow caught the rows of books – history, wars and military campaigns. This man wasn't stupid. He had a sharp brain; deprived of any schooling, but nevertheless quite learned.

"Oi understand you're joinin' up, lad?" Abram's voice jarred his thoughts.

"Yes … yes, I'm enlisting in the army."

He'd noticed him looking at the militaria on the shelves. Maybe this was a sign of approval.

"Wal you're a fule then, bu' then you're young so you're entitled to be. Oi stayed on the land. Oi woos needed there like many; no' like moi dad and his relations; thay were thur unlucky ones. Poor Harry, he woos thur firs'. Gassed in noo man's land. He navver stood a chance. All young fules thay were. You can still gi' killed yow know – gorn orff to war, even nowadays in such far flung places like Iraq and 'ghanistan."

He rubbed his stubbly chin. "Is tha' why you took such an interes' in my Izzy?"

He didn't wait for an answer. "Oi saw you lookin' a' her bum, coorved fresh and firm as peaches.

A qook prize a' fore you're orff playin' a' soldiers? She's very impressionable, jist like her mother res' her soul. She's no' simple, she jist prefers thur simple ways 'f life so you respec' her!"

He wasn't far-off the mark if he was honest. Abram was shrewd, that much was obvious. He had first met Izzy last summer while taking a stroll along the beach just a stone's throw down the coast. A small, lithe figure darting hither and thither among the shingle and sand; her wind tossed hair dancing in the breeze and the gusts wrapping her garments tightly round her frame. She was all bright colours and she shone in the sunlight. She had greeted him with a smile of innocence and her face was fresh and devoid of paint, which seemed to complement her naked calves and feet splashing through the brine.

"I'm collecting flotsam and jetsam," she explained, and she placed a wicker basket in front of him cluttered with driftwoods, seaweed, shells and stones awash with colours and worn smooth by the sea. "All have their uses to someone. They're sold as curios in the shops and stalls in the town, and besides, we need the money, my uncle and I."

Yes it was true, he had seen her as a prize to begin with; something to satisfy him before he ran away and played soldiers. So far the prize had eluded him, but it no longer mattered; he had grown rather fond of her. There was a kind of wisdom about her masked behind the innocence, which imbued intelligence and thoughtfulness.

"Don't go and play at soldiers." It was she who

had coined the phrase only days after they had met. Thoughtfulness and concern, yes. Love? Perhaps.

The legion of Roman chess pieces on a table in the corner of the room glowed red by the firelight. Their faces glowered at him warlike, as though to re-emphasise her words.

That night he dreamed. It must have been the book that Abram had handed to him without a word as he took his leave and returned to his digs. Before he entered that half sleeping, half waking world, he remembered snuggling under the bedclothes and staring up at the skylight of the sloping roofed window above his bed. He'd finished the first page, because its contents lingered in his mind after he had extinguished the lamp and entered the realm of darkness ....

"If by chance you have occasion to travel along the old Roman road in North Norfolk known as Peddars Way, then beware, for the peace and tranquillity pervading this quiet, rural idyll may be brutally awakened by the spectral appearance of a phantom black dog.

"The brute may strike at any time upon the weary and unsuspecting traveller as they make their way across the leafy glades and cornfields, and many such cases have been reported, even in recent times. They can appear at gateways, entrances, and crossroads. At Roundham Cross, north east of Thetford for instance, a motorist encountered a huge dog, which crossed in front of him as it appeared out of the early morning mist. He braced himself, expecting to feel the sickening thud against the wing of the car, and was surprised when no such crunch occurred; even more so,

when he spotted the phantom reappear on the other side, still stalking the line of the ancient trackway.

"Massingham Heath too, is notorious for the haunting, and once on a chill October morning when the trees were bare, a hiker reported a savage black dog, "with vicious eyes, red and bloodshot, and filled with hate", running towards him, "with great speed". It leapt upon him, but as he covered his face with his arm in sheer terror, the dog never struck him; it had vanished into the cold, crisp air. Later, so the newspaper report said, the unfortunate man became involved in an accident at sea and drowned, and so reinforced the belief that a sighting of this canine ghostly form spelt a portent of doom."

The book dropped from the bed.

Then came the breathing.

Slow and rhythmic at first, but awful.

Wheezing, resonating.

Above him. Beside him … close up and next to him.

His own slumbering breath, and yet outside of him … away from his body, but close by.

It grew louder, rasping and jarring on his breastbone.

No air. No air. Suffocating.

All was black. Where was the light?

Oh, so black, suffocating …

And a putrid smell. His nose burned, so did his chest; it tightened, constricting his airways.

His stomach contorted as he wretched. He fought for breath, fought for air, heaving desperate …

At last he found the light switch, and he was left with the sound of his own respiring; no other, and slower now … and easier.

Now, he slept with the light on.

***

A fresh wind blew, perfumed with an aroma of brine and seaweed, which suffused into his lungs. A fickle sun shone high, and hues of yellow and blue glimmered around him. The surf and shiny wet pebbles glistened across golden sand as the sea retreated towards the horizon. Its roar receded as the gulls screeched timelessly.

He raised his hand to his brow and squinted at the skyline; the blinding glare pulsed and flashed as the scudding clouds broke. Izzy was out there foraging, Abram had said so. She had left his cottage before breakfast in order to catch the retreating tide and so gather the flotsam and jetsam.

For a moment he thought he saw her - the small, wiry windswept figure with smock and hair flapping just like the first time he'd met her - but a dose of sand and flies whipped at his face and blinded him. He flinched and she was gone; disappeared somewhere among the dunes, behind the beached fishing boat, or roaming the flats.

Somewhere … nowhere.

The outline of Saint Mary's still brooded on the spit of land, but now it was the morning haze and not clammy fog that shrouded its features. He thought of the hound slumbering in its glass tomb.

He remembered her placing her delicate hand on his breast. "Don't go; don't be a soldier …no."

Those eyes when she uttered her plea, and her tone so warm, trusting, and wise.

He headed for the shoreline.

Ooom … Ooom

The muffled, eerie sound of the bitterns out over the tidal creek pounded the ether. The church and spire dulled again as the encompassing rain clouds smothered the sun, and the gulls screeched and circled, their cries more agitated. The wind whipped up the sand so that it swirled and hit his face with stinging stabs.

It was cold; the tide was returning and so was the mist. Its grey tendrils were closing in on the beach and heading straight for him with astonishing speed.

"Izzy?" He shouted uselessly into the breeze and his calls were drowned by the huffs and sighs of the advancing waves.

The rate of the incoming fog alarmed him. He decided he'd better retreat before he lost his sense of direction, but as he clambered up a steep bank of shingle away from the sand, the crest eluded him. His breathing became laboured, a noise so familiar, along with another ….

Ooom … Ooom

Louder now. At last he reached the top of the ridge. The gorse and dunes ahead were already dissolving into greyness as the swirling haar engulfed them. It was then that he became aware of crunching footsteps behind him.

"Izzy?"

No, the steps were too heavy. Someone else was out there with him, and approaching from the invisible shoreline. He turned but there was nothing but a wall of grey. Yet the footsteps were closing in – *crunch crunch.*

He had to get away. He tottered down the shingle towards the drier dunes and gorse but he lost his footing and tripped. The stones cut his palms as he reached out to break his fall. He clutched at his smarting wrist and lay flat on his stomach. He twisted round and gazed up the stony ridge from where he had stumbled, waiting for the stalker to manifest ….

A blackened, rounded head appeared from behind the crest's summit. It hesitated momentarily when it spotted him. What was left of the feeble sunlight sharpened its silhouette in the opaque, enveloping fog.

Its body emerged – upright, vaguely human – and it scrambled down the bank towards him, wielding a stick in its fist; an act played out in dreadful slow-motion. It laboured, it wheezed, it staggered.

Boom … boom clatter clatter.

Panic welled up inside him. He picked himself up and criss-crossed the dunes, taking careful steps – the worst thing he could do would be to run. He should be able to outpace his pursuer, so long as he kept his sense of direction.

But the sand beneath his feet turned sticky and wet, and his legs felt heavy. Surely he hadn't strayed onto the flats.

No … another bank to climb, but this wasn't

sand … it was mud!

Boom … boom bang clatter bang.

Yellow will'o the wisps sparked over the vista. Marsh gas?

The writhing fog had changed; no longer freezing and clammy, but hot and dry, acrid and smoky - it burned. Not marsh gas, but *mustard gas*.

His strength was failing and as he fought for breath, his mouth gaped and his tongue protruded. The booms and bangs and clatters deafened him.

Rat-a-tat, rat-a-tat.

Yells and screeches from every direction; spitting gunfire, howls of pain and anguish so deafening, and voices screeched and yelled from all around. They pleaded and they cried, and tearfully, he thought and longed for Izzy.

He fell to his knees; he was done. Flames burned at his skin and boulders of mud spewed into the air as the ground thundered and shook. The smell … he clutched at his chest, riven with pain, and gasped and gasped and gasped. Soon he would suffocate.

The figure - the monster - scrambled up the bank, closing in on him, heaving and wheezing in time with his own labouring - desperate for breath, desperate for life - until it collapsed almost on top of him. Its large, bulbous head rested close to his cheek. At last he understood what he saw. The top of the head was a helmet, steel and circular, and the face a mask. There were no eyes discernible, just roundels of glass. One hand of the dead soldier clutched at the respirator on his chest, while the other still gripped on the rifle. A tongue protruded from the blackened lips, and for a moment he glimpsed the eyes from behind the glass covered holes, or at least the whites, for the pupils were rolled back.

Then the smoke and the burning closed in and the cacophony of the battlefield embraced him, *consumed* him … and he felt nothing.

***

He must have lain there for a long time – how long, he couldn't tell – but slowly the deep sighs of the sea swell lapping onto the shoreline from beyond the shingle bank revived him. It fed his mind, reviving his senses … the wondrous light of the sky with its radiance of yellows and blues filtering through his eyelids …. And when he opened them all was calm. The breeze caressed him. With his strength returning, he rose and brushed the sand from him as he climbed back up the bank. The midday sun coloured the ocean a dazzling, sparkling blue, and the azure was still and cloudless.

He rested and gazed, and after a while retraced his steps to the church. On the way he did some thinking about the portent he'd witnessed. Maybe the army was a bad idea; instead he would search and find Izzy again no matter how long it took.

Once inside the church, he paid his respects at the war memorial.

Black Shuck still slept, but this time he made sure he paid his penny – in fact he placed all his coin into the collection box.

The Ridgeway, West Berkshire

The ancient track known as The Ridgeway is a paradise for explorers wishing to delve into the history and folklore of the hillforts, burial mounds and prehistoric monuments scattered along the way.

One such curiosity, an Iron Age barrow, purports to contain treasure, and bears the amusing name, 'Scutchamer Knob', and is hidden within a leafy copse. I was disappointed to find it littered with the detritus of what looked like a party of miscreant youths. However, it did provide the inspiration for this disturbing tale.

Rude Awakening

I've just had a god-awful nightmare.

I dreamed about a huge mound of grass and earth looming at me in front of a dark and thunderous sky. A hand poked out of the top and wriggled and twitched, desperate to get free. I tried to help and I scratched and clawed at the soil until my fingers bled and my heart pumped. Her body fell onto me; her flesh still supple on my fingertips and yet clammy, grimy and cold. She stank, and her dead eyes stared at me accusingly. Behind her in the chamber of stone and earth, ancient, disarticulated skeletons were strewn across the floor, stained with age, entangled by tree roots and embedded in the mud. Scurrying rats infested them as they emerged, panic-stricken and searching desperately for new hideaways.

I know what caused it – dozing in the heat of the afternoon sun by this hummock …

I'd parked the car up on Bury Down and wandered along The Ridgeway path without a care for the time, or where my meanderings would take me. I breathed in the warm balmy air, and rejoiced at the freedom of the open landscape. Not even the distant stream of traffic, its roar no more than a sigh, and glistening from the sun shining in the valley far below me, could break the spell.

And such colours too – the glowing beige and yellows of the corn fields, the wild flowers in the hedgerow, and a deep blue sky from which a scattering of gleaming white clouds bubbled. Of course, the humidity had made me tire easily, but as the clump of trees on the horizon appeared ahead, I quickened my pace, for there was shelter.

But my progress had been slow… agonisingly so. I squinted into the haze, my eyes sore from the streaming sunrays. Why weren't the trees getting any closer?

I plodded, eventually arriving alongside a copse and a broken, weatherworn sign, resembling a gnarled finger pointing into a dense thicket of beech and elder. The words, robbed by time, meant something to me.

Well, I had to enter – into the coolness, away from the blinding blaze of the sun, and towards the welcoming darkness of the boughs and trunks of the spinney.

I wandered aimlessly, until the large circular mound caught me unawares from out of the gloom. The cluster of oddly perched trees crowning its flattened summit looked down at me like watching sentinels, guarding the hummock and whatever secrets it held.

It certainly didn't look natural.

… And then I remembered the map back in the car and that funny name - Scutchamer Knob - and I suddenly realised where I was. It was supposed to be the location of King Alfred's famous victory over the invading Vikings, but was, in fact, a prehistoric round barrow; a burial from the Iron Age.

The sentinels watched over me in the stillness and silence of the shaded enclosure with malignance, affronted by my intrusion, and stark against a backdrop of open fields and a bright, rolling terrain. That's where I collapsed onto its grassy bank and closed my eyes and began to doze ….

I opened them momentarily - a distant rumble of thunder - but the dazzling whiteness of the cow parsley and the red poppies shimmering in the heat and haze over the vista, made me close them again.

Of course I fell asleep.

Of course I had the nightmare …

A second rumble of thunder - louder, more angry this time - had awoken me, and here I sit ….

I gaze at the horizon. From there the clouds diffuse - they *creep* - like ink slowly tainting a pure sky; black clouds blotting the white; dark and malignant.

The skylarks no longer sing. I shiver, in spite of the humid air.

The approaching maelstrom is still some distance, and here, the intensity of the sun prevails and beats down on me. I'm drowsy, I want to sleep, but … its orange, incandescent glow filtering through my closed eyelids extinguishes unexpectedly.

"Hey, Mister … s'cuse me, Mister, I need help."

The jarring, intrusive voice makes me jump. I jerk backwards and hit my head on the wall of the mound.

I blink, my heart pounds; a big face looms, youthful and staring – a female.

"I'm sorry, luv, I didn't mean to startle you."

She stands up straight and edges back a little. She must have sprung from round the curve of the mound where I lie.

"It's OK," I stammer, "it's just that you crept up on me. I didn't hear you approach … no footsteps … I thought I was quite alone out here."

I feel vulnerable; she may have backed off, but she's still staring down at me. She could do anything … pull a knife.

She can't be more than eighteen, twenty at most – I notice freckles, juxtaposing the tight hipster jeans that outline her shapely legs and hips. And that striped rugby shirt is unbuttoned a little too much; it reveals her ample chest … she's no innocent. But the red open toed high heels are odd – they don't belong.

She doesn't belong, not out here.

"We've 'bin camping - me and my boyfriend."

She points towards the woods beyond the hump, but I see nothing; nothing but darkness and shadows amid the trees.

She brushes her raven hair from her eyes, so that the long, untidy locks straggle her neck and breasts. She's perspiring; her face is grimy and with a hardened expression; there's a look of alarm about her.

"He's a pig. All he wants me to do is cook n' things. He didn't tell me his mates were comin' along. I'm not playin' their games, especially when night comes. They've gone off to town to fetch beer and ciggies, so I'm leggin' it!"

Another rumble of thunder. I glance at the sweeping landscape; the inky clouds are spewing across the sky, causing the world to darken, and yet her visage stays unnaturally bright, defying the dissolving sunlight.

The stillness, the mugginess, *she,* makes me uneasy.

"You all right?" I ask rather stupidly.

"Oh yes, luv, I can look after m'self. It's just that I'd rather go now while he's out of sight. Is that your car back there?"

"Er, yes on Bury Down … but it's quite a hike."

This isn't right. You can't even see my car from here. How long has she been following me without my knowing?

"If you could jus' give me a lift to the village,

and I'll make my own way from there."

We walk through the woods and head for the track. I throw a second glance at where she had pointed, but there's no sign of a tent or anything. I lag behind and can't stop looking at those legs and hips striding in front of me.

"We'd better get a move on n'case he gets back sooner; he's got a bit of a temper."

I curse. This is all I need.

And time's playing tricks on me as well. One moment we're at the broken sign by the edge of the copse, and the next we're traversing The Ridgeway, where the ground is open, grassy and rutted, and the trees are diminishing into a blob on the distant skyline. Or, perhaps it's because I've been too busy ogling her; she *is* gorgeous after all. She struggles as she hurries in those red heeled shoes; they catch in the ruts. Is she worried about the approaching rainstorm – the sky growls moodily again – or *him*? What *is* she doing out here?

The land slopes away to the east of us into a huge depression; I know it as 'Grim's Dyke'. I can see my car in the distance, but it's shrouded in shadow. The storm has got there first and is heading our way, so we're in for a soaking. She steps up her pace – those long legs – and I have difficulty keeping up with her in this airless, sticky heat. My breaths are stunted.

The poppies have bowed their heads, saddened by the passing of the skylarks. They are preparing for the approaching tumult.

Now she's walking alongside and looking at me … and within a blink of my eye.

"My name's Roxanne, but everyone calls me Roxy. Gaz - that's my boyfriend - he's just a kid, but you … I go for blokes like you … you've got your head screwed on… the kind sort, knows 'ow to treat a girl."

Funny, she seems older now; perhaps it's the shifting light patterns caused by the rolling clouds. Those huge brown eyes study me, but with an air of world-weariness ahead of her years; a hardened, cynical, expression, I'd say.

"Oh, just give me a lift to the service station on the main road, luv. I gotta a mate there, he'll help me." There is disappointment in her tone, as though she's expecting something from me.

The storm clouds draw near; a rumble, a flash of lightning, adding to my unease, *my fear*. Yes … *something isn't right.*

"But you don't even know me, I could be anyone." My excuse, my apology.

She stares, a more twisted smile morphing on her lips.

"Oh, I *do* know you … luv."

***

I sit bolt upright. Everywhere's so black and suffocating as I frantically fumble for the light switch, clutching my chest, gasping for breath. The gentle gleam calms me as I reach for the glass of water by my bedside. I'm soaked through - no rainstorm, but a fit of the night sweats. I glance at the familiar surrounds of the bedroom; it reassures and comforts me. What a nightmare that was; the mound, the girl …

A faint tap at the door. It opens slightly and Jack emerges from the hall. The backlight from the hallway casts his face in shadow; the glare mimics the sun in my dream and causes me to squint. I'm unable to make out his features, or his expression … except for the glint in his eyes.

"All right, old son? Heard you shout."

He steps into the room hesitantly, not wishing to intrude.

"Yes, I'm OK, just a bad dream."

"Want to talk about it?"

"No I'm fine, it's already fading."

I'm starting to feel better. He's a fine chap is Uncle Jack, very helpful. He seems so contented since he retired and moved to the country and keen to enjoy the good things in life: walking, swimming, fishing, good food and fine wine. Of course, he'd been all at sea when Aunt Jen had died, but since he met Sophie and remarried, well, it may have caused a few tongues to wag, what with the age difference and so on, but it's definitely given him a new lease of life. I'd be lost if I couldn't visit for a few days each summer because there's something about the rolling landscape of Wiltshire and the Berkshire downs that draws me.

"Maybe we'll get a long walk in tomorrow," he says, the backlight illuminating his shock of white hair. "The three of us, and perhaps we'll stop off for a pub lunch.

"Anyway, it's so humid tonight, Sophie's making some iced tea; it might help us to sleep more restfully. So, as well as being young and adorable, she's thoughtful too. Here she comes …."

As Jack leaves the room a feeling of calm imbues me. I love this bedroom, especially the oak bookcase over in the corner with its maps and old books copiously filled with tales of legend and folklore. During previous visits, when the weather was inclement, I'd while away the hours turning their pages, and when the rain had passed, I'd be off exploring whichever prehistoric barrow, monolith or medieval churchyard listed therein had fired my imagination.

I notice one of the tomes lying on the floor next to my bed. I must have been thumbing through it before turning out the lamp and falling asleep. I stretch my arm, and nestle into the pillow. Yes … a map of The Ridgeway near Bury Down, with all those strange sounding names scattered upon it: 'World's End', 'Grim's Dyke', 'Scutchamer Knob'.

'Scutchamer Knob …'Scutch …

I remember.

I sense a movement by the doorway. Sophie? A figure in silhouette outlined by the light from the hallway is watching me, shattering the tranquillity. She approaches, my chest tightens. She's wearing a low-cut nightgown, upon which a cascade of long raven hair hangs lank. The lamplight casts a sultry glow on her ample bosom. She has a youthful expression, and her big brown eyes are studying me as she holds the tray.

"Your iced tea … luv."

***

I lurch, twitch, and bang my head on the inside roof of the car. It's as though an electric charge has shot right through me. I curse; my whole body aches. I must have fallen asleep after that interminable hike back from … somewhere.

Torrential rain is beating on the windows making it impossible for me to see outside. It was probably the sudden force of the downpour that woke me. I've just had the strangest of dreams; I'd actually dreamed that I was staying at Uncle Jack's … but that was from a time long since past - years in fact. I was sitting in bed in the guest room and surrounded by those dusty old maps and books, but something had frightened me … something …

I'll wait until the storm abates, after which the air will be clear and fresh again. Then I'll go for a stroll before driving back to my digs.

The rain continues to pelt and spew - thudding, staccato beats hammering on the pane - blasting in torrents. I wipe away my misty breath upon the glass, peering into the grey murk.

THUMP.

I lurch again, jarring my neck.

A piercing scream. A face presses against the window, palms beating at the glass.

"Help, HELP … let me in … Please, PLEASE

HELP ME!"

Roxy; I'd forgotten about her.

I cower, wishing she would go away.

Her visage, ghastly white, and hands poking through the deluge; her eyes wide with terror, and smears of mascara staining her cheeks. Rain splashes off her soaked, matted hair.

She screams, mouth gaping.

THUMP THUMP THUMP.

"Please let me in … *please*, HE'LL KILL ME!"

THUMP THUMP.

She screams once more. Her head jerks back and the curtain of water engulfs her, leaving only her pressing palms. Then, they just melt in the downpour; they slide down the pane slowly and silently. There's nothing now but the din of the torrent. I dare to breathe.

A muffled splat and the face reappears, pressed against the glass, but only for a moment. No thumping, no scream … just wide, lifeless eyes, with mouth and lips contorted and grotesque, and running mascara mingling with rich, red blood. It dilutes and washes away into the deluge of the storm. The dead face hovers - black, staring eyes - until it slithers down, out of sight.

I clamp my hands round me, burying my head in my lap as I try desperately to obliterate the horrible spectre. My heart pounds, and the rattle of the rainstorm persists, uninterrupted ….

I remain coiled like a foetus, rocking, with hands clamped on ears, seeking oblivion; I don't really know how long for.

The mist has cleared off the window. The storm's passed, and a bright, golden early evening sun shines from the west. What a relief; suddenly I no longer feel threatened. I step out of the car.

There's nothing out here; no sign of a struggle or anything; it all seems so peaceful. I must have been dreaming ….

The wetted land glistens, bathing the sloping downs with spots of crystal. The light bounces off the cars on the busy road far below me. I breathe in the ozone.

But I'm up here all alone, on this high ridge.

I notice an object beneath the driver's door – a tatty, red high-heeled shoe, spattered with mud.

***

I gasp, my eyes rip open and strain into the blackness as I try to catch my breath. I'm drenched – the night sweats again.

Wait … the bedside clock ticks softly by my side.

Ha!

I smile, then snigger with relief. I reach for the bedside lamp and look down at the tangle of sheets joyously. My wardrobe opposite greets me, *comforts* me, with my newly pressed suit and shirt hanging from the handle, all ready for the morning.

It's 4 a.m.

I shake my head, musing over the dream that I'd just had. The Ridgeway, the wood, that weird burial mound, and the girl … that sexy girl. And then there was old Uncle Jack, but that was many, many years ago, I was young ….

Dreams within dreams.

And *so* vivid, but as with every dream, it will fade, such is its ephemeral nature.

Soft footsteps creaking on the stairs … another reassuring, familiar sound. I switch off the light and pretend to be asleep for I know that's what she would prefer. I could tell her about the dream tomorrow.

I watch the graceful form glide … a lithe, beautiful shimmer across the darkened room and with a gentle rustling of the sheets, she enters the bed. Her face is turned away towards the wall - something that occurs all too often now - but her scent intoxicates me, filling my senses, and a tear forms in my eye. I gaze longingly at the graceful neck, the arch of her back and the narrow waist, and the sheer beauty of the feminine shape beside me.

But … this isn't right either; no, it isn't right at all.

I'm not thinking straight. My wife … well, she's gone … she went a long time ago.

What's wrong with me?

Quickly, I switch the light back on. I place my palm on her shoulder and she turns to face me. A large, pale visage looms close to me amid the dingy tungsten glow, one with big brown eyes, freckles, and framed by long raven hair …

"All right, luv?"

I scream.

***

I feel like 'shite!

I stand abruptly. What a stupid thing to do, dozing off like that beside this barrow. The grass beneath me is all squashed and moist, and the water's soaked through to my skin. My face is dry and itchy from sunburn.

And what of the dream … that endless dream? I look around me nervously, half expecting her to appear from behind the curve of the mound … that girl Roxy …

No, everything seems normal …

Best to get away from here now that I've come to my senses at last; now that I'm truly awake, because otherwise I'll start to think that I'm going mad.

I hurry from that weird hump of earth with those strange guardian trees watching over me. I glimpse something from the corner of my eye … a splash of orange not too far into the woods. I walk into the darkness, my nerves frayed, but I have to see, I *have* to.

Then I realise what it is - a bivouac; it looks abandoned and weather-beaten.

The tent is battered and torn and there's a musty air of dripping damp and mould. Empty beer cans, plastic food cartons, syringes and other detritus tell a story of miscreant youth and aggression. A broken heeled red shoe lies partially hidden by the flap at the entrance.

Alarm bells sound within me. I try to reassure

myself – maybe I had spotted it earlier and it had caused me to dream about the girl. But as I approach, the eerie gloom envelops me. I feel so melancholy…

The sense of despair overwhelms me ….

I remember – I remember – I remember.

I should have helped her, but as always I just ran away.

I failed her, as I had with my wife many years ago when I should have shown more kindness, more understanding. Instead I drove her to leave. She never told me she was going, she simply disappeared. I tried to tell her I cared but …

And then there was Sophie, Jack's young bride. I still feel awful and ashamed about what happened, but well, we *had* drank too much wine … that and the aroma of her intoxicating perfume and the low-cut gown – that's what made me do it. I leant too close, felt the caress of her silky hair on my skin, and I kissed her beneath her ear, upon her neck … a lingering kiss, just long enough to be a betrayal. Jack tried to forgive me, he tried so hard, but I couldn't go there anymore, no …

First my wife, then Sophie; it was my fault, as was this, this incident, this *fixation* with Roxy. And so much worse.

"You're standing behind me and watching me … reading my thoughts, aren't you, Roxy? I know you are there." My voice echoes hollow among the trees. Only they seem to answer as they sway and sigh in the breeze.

But she *is* here. I know because I remember it all

now.

… the ambulance up on Bury Down; the lights flashing and the paramedics lifting the lifeless form onto a stretcher as a dark, mud spattered lock of raven hair slid from the body bag.

I am *so* sorry, Roxy. I should have let you into the car and drove you to safety but I was too scared. I shall never forget your face pressed against the glass pleading for help and yet I left you …I left you to die.

I can't forget … I can't forget.

And I think about the old book of folklore in Jack's room, which described how our ancient ancestors used to bury their dead in those strange mounds of earth like the one out there … the way they used to dig them up again and again so that their spirits could roam freely and talk to them, and impart their guidance and wisdom. Well, what happened when, through the aeons of time, no-one believed in that sort of thing anymore? Who could all those spirits of the dead, those phantoms, talk to then?

… Unless someone like me comes along.

Something makes the hairs on my nape prickle. She's here with me right now. I turn around.

"Hey, Mister …'scuse me, Mister, I need help."

My throat tightens as I scream and scream and scream.

Nevern Churchyard, Dyfed

Yews are an ancient species of tree and live to a great age. They were regarded as sacred by pagans and are often found in Christian graveyards, land previously revered by followers of earlier deities. No wonder then that yew trees are the source of many a ghostly account.

One of the yews at Nevern exudes a reddish sap and some believe this to be the blood of a monk hanged in the churchyard for crimes he did not commit.

My visit there inspired this tale.

Bleeding Hearts

The numbing rain beat hard upon them as they stood together on a grassy mound under the shelter of the ancient yew tree. Low-lying globules of clouds pulsed across the sky, spewing their flux over the burial ground with ice-cold breaths, and dulling the tangle of ivy and gravestones before them with pallors of grey.

Thomas averted his gaze from the sodden earth to his master's face hidden behind the cowl … except for the familiar protruding greying beard, the lined cheeks and the square jaw.

"Soon, young novice Thomas, soon …" The huge man nodded stoically, defying the rough discomfort of the monk's habit, his bearing determined and articulate.

The two workmen below laboured with picks

and spades, digging and clawing, their mood sullen. An invisible rook's caw echoed above from somewhere within the leafy canopy.

The rainwater dripped and splashed from the lush greenery of the yew onto Thomas's head. It dribbled from his thickset, youthful hair into his eyes.

"You should follow my example and raise your cowl," Father Simons retorted, his stare fixed on the macabre exhumation. "Have my teachings not even taught you some basic common sense?"

He turned to Thomas and for the first time that morning the youth caught the benevolent twinkle in his master's eye. It reassured him as a gentle, mocking smile formed on the rugged man's lips. "All that water running from your downy mane and onto your fresh-faced skin – you look like a girl ..."

But his smile dropped abruptly – a single, deliberate act, reminding Thomas of his wrong-doing. "And that's why we're here – to purge these inclinations you have for this girl ... if that's what she is."

"But, Father, isn't that what our Lord teaches us ... to love?"

"Not when you're a novice from the Cistercian order of monks, my boy." His eyebrow rose. "Our Lord teaches us a different form of love, certainly not the pleasures of the flesh."

A cry of disgust from the workmen interrupted them. They edged back from the trench grimacing, turning their heads away.

Father Simons stepped purposefully down from

the mound and studied the open grave with a resigned air. Thick, black treacle mixed with mud and rotting splinters of coffin wood formed a soup in the soil. "And that, young Thomas, is our fleshes' truest form ... The Lord decrees."

Thomas stepped from the shelter reluctantly. He stood by the grey bearded cleric and peered into the pit, trying to discern the nature of the detritus inside. Human remains bubbled in the oily gloop - a glutinous mess of disarticulated skeletal limbs and ribs, stained brown, and entwined by the roots of the yew. They glistened as they caught the weak light emanating from the brightening sky.

"See how the roots of the yew resemble tendrils of a demon, as though it's drawing all the poor human souls towards its heart. No wonder the pagans worshipped the yew tree and the underworld - the world beneath our feet."

A gobbet of mud slithered down the side of the trench exposing a skull. A rootlet clasped it through the eye-socket and a worm slipped from the lower jaw. Thomas recoiled and felt the bile rise in his gullet. He covered his mouth with his fist, heaving at the stench of death and rotted matter.

"... our flesh's truest form ... The Lord decrees."

The big man seemed oblivious. "You'll often find yew trees in cemeteries ... they pre-date the graves themselves. Pagans worshipped them and believed they drew the dead souls from the earth into the wood, limbs and fibre of the tree's very being ... and witnessing this, you can understand why."

He gazed up at the firmament, muttering, and

waiting for the glimmer of sunlight to dispel the darkness of the rain clouds. "But that's not why we're here."

He looked down again, prodding at what Thomas took to be a moist lump of clay with his staff. A dark red liquid oozed from within.

"What is it, Master? A dead rodent? Sap from the tree? I've heard legends—"

Father Simons waved his arm, silencing him. He lifted the mass of slop into the air with the staff. It throbbed with life and pulsated. Worse, Thomas watched the rugged, dependable expression of his mentor flinch as he flung it back into the grave. It seemed to burrow in the direction of the yew's bole.

"Hearts … human hearts, novice Thomas, from the souls of those committed to the earth, and never having reached heaven … kept alive and pumping blood in homage to the pagan spirit that dwells in that ancient yew."

Now Thomas realised what the sticky sap seeping from the russet gnarled bark meant, and he grimaced at his brown stained palm in horror. Earlier he had rested his hand on an open sore of the trunk and the reddened, congealing goo had coated his skin. Blood! He recoiled, retreated to the adjacent tree and wretched up the contents of his stomach into the grass. His master left him be, not through callousness but because he loved him and was allowing him a little dignity, sinful though that was. After all, his mentor was subjecting him to this ordeal for a purpose, even though the reason eluded him. He had grown to depend on Father Simons ever since he was wrenched away from the bosom of his dying mother amid the poverty, squalor and despair of the workhouse. He was all he knew.

He heard Father Simons issue a command for the gravediggers to continue with their work. "I want you to disturb as much of the earth around these old graves as you can … to the cemetery's boundary where it meets the riverbank. It is necessary if we are to catch her."

Thomas waited for the approaching footsteps of the figure in the rough Cistercian habit. It sat beside him and placed a large reassuring hand on his shoulder.

"Master, isn't what you're doing sacrilege … exhuming the dead … against our holy teachings?"

"It *is*, Thomas, but they, the priests and the clergy, always call on me to do this kind of thing. Indeed, I've been expelled, excommunicated and even imprisoned in the past - such ingratitude - but they always forgive me when they want it doing all over again."

"Doing what? And are those hearts weeping blood really alive? And what did you mean when you said, 'if we are to catch her'?"

"One thing at a time, my boy."

He pulled the cowl from his head and revealed his thick, silvery mane. The burgeoning light caught the blue eyes and the wisdom that emanated from them.

"But first, I need you to tell me about the girl.

You must tell me, Thomas."

They both rested by the trunk of the tree, this one of oak. Here at least, it was comparatively dry. He wiped his palm on his robe, drew two small loaves and flagons from the pocket of his habit and handed Thomas his share.

"Well," Thomas began, "about a week ago I arrived here at the chapel to perform my duties. It was dusk, just before Vespers, and I saw someone watching me - an elfin, timid figure - moving in the twilight and shadows over here by the yew tree. I think it was foraging the ground, and it appeared to be putting things into its mouth. A beggar, I assumed, driven by starvation into scavenging for roots and fallen berries.

"Then, two men appeared and started harassing her. I knew it to be a woman by her pitiful cries and pleas. I approached and shouted, and, seeing I was of holy orders, they retreated back to the village. I reached out my arm and helped her to her feet. Her hand clasped mine … it seemed so small and delicate … and her face …. Father, I have never seen such innocence and beauty. It shone from behind the grime and the despair."

The wise man sniffed. "Young and foolish boy."

"She uttered no words, but I gave her the food I carried. She looked at me with tears of gratitude, and my heart wept with her. She turned and disappeared among the foliage and gravestones."

"You didn't see where she went? Where she returned to?"

"No, Father."

"And why do you suppose the men attacked her?"

"Why to force themselves on her … to obtain her favours. I felt for her. She is as I was - alone, with no-one - and a beggar. Master, I cannot understand your lack of Christian humility."

"Tell me, Thomas, does any of this explain your subsequent alacrity in returning to your dormitory after performing your duties at the chapel?" The question was rhetorical. "Come now, my son, I must know all of it if I am to do what I have to do."

Thomas bowed his head, feeling his master's disapproval.

"Well … I took her bread every evening after Vespers, sometimes at night after Compline, and we met by the yew tree. She never spoke; she just knew I would be there. And last time, she held out her hand and she touched my face … she stroked my cheek and gazed at me. She understood.

"I could feel lustful stirrings within, but I couldn't help myself. She pushed me gently onto the ground and sat across my lap, legs astride me. She leant forward and kissed me in a sinful way. Her lips and her hair were so soft, the like of which I can only remember as an infant - but this was somehow different. She unbuttoned her garments and took my hand and pressed it to her flesh … to her breast. How could such smoothness of the flesh, such warmth, *such beauty*, even among the squalor and grime, be ungodly, Master?

"She continued to kiss me, and more passionately. She was making strange noises and moving her hips – grinding them onto mine. I knew it was wrong and I could feel myself stirring but it seemed to increase her vigour, and … and, well you know…"

Thomas faltered; his master was as impassive as ever. If he hadn't known his mentor better, he would swear that he had simply lost interest. "Father, do you hear me? I'm certain that I love her."

But there was no answer; instead, he was gazing at the sky, and towards the open expanse beyond the riverbank. A sunray pierced through a break in the clouds, banishing the greyness and gloom; a streak of gold, bathing the distant hills purple, and catching the moment of triumph in his beady, blue eyes.

"There, Thomas, do you see it … now that the rain clouds have broke? That's what I wanted to show you! Do you perceive the standing stones … there amongst the gorse and the pools of water?"

The vista of moors and scrub had erupted into luminescent greens and mauves, and in the distance, a ring of megaliths – pale blue-white fangs – protruded from the earth.

"*That's* where she comes from, Thomas, not the village. Those men were driving her *away* from their folk. You see, long ago, before this land was blessed by the teachings of our Lord, the people worshipped false gods – demons, you could say. All sorts of ungodly acts occurred here and that's why our forefathers built our places of worship on these heretical sites, just like the one here." He pointed to the chapel. "But these yew trees and the circle of stone, and the so-called spirits that dwell in the river, were here a long time before our Christian forbears.

"There have been rumours of a demon dwelling around here for centuries, that's why they've called me here … for my unorthodox ways. It takes the guise of an enchanting female - probably a soul it claimed from one of the many virgins sacrificed at the stone circle from thousands of years ago - and dwells among the yews and shadows seeking its prey - innocents such as you, my boy."

"But why would our forbears carry out such barbarous and heinous acts … and on women?"

"To sacrifice the flower of their offspring.They believed that by spilling her blood and allowing it to seep into the earth, it would bring fertility to the land, thus providing the fruits of food and offspring to their people."

Thomas shuddered. "Then, I have had intercourse with The Devil. I am lost."

"Not The Devil, but have fortitude. She's no longer human, but a tormented soul that never accepted her fate and with no-one to guide her to Saint Peter. She is doomed to feed on the flesh and blood of the living. A ghoul … a demon!"

Simons glanced towards the reed beds and the river, biting his lip, contemplating. "I wonder …"

Tendrils of weeds twisted lazily in the muddy flow of the current. Droplets of rain agitated the surface making the submerged fronds sway and writhe a little more than they should. His eagle blue eyes sparked again. "Yes!" Something hidden broke the water's surface and the reeds stirred.

"A water sprite … she's taken the form of a water sprite!" He crouched and poised his staff like a weapon as he peered into the undergrowth.

"Master?"

"They're particularly fond of human hearts, you know," he added with a dreadful whisper. "Remember the grave?" He forced his hand on his protégé's shoulder, cutting short any further questioning and compelling Thomas to cower close to his teacher and protector. He watched the raindrops dance upon the surface of the pool, their patter punctuating the awful stillness.

A rustle among the reeds, a quiver amid the russet red boughs of the yew …

"There! Right beside us, Thomas. We must act with stealth." Simons reached for a spade nearby, abandoned by the absent gravediggers.

"Yes … a water sprite; our digging for bodies has lured it," he sibilated, gritting his teeth as the rain glistened on his beard.

A vicious, screeching scowl – the green of the yew parted, and the creature, half woman, half feline, burst and pounced on them; a black-green blur of a beast on all-fours, hissing through its spiked teeth.

"It's come out of nowhere." Thomas cried and toppled back.

"No, from Hell!" Simons hurled his staff like a javelin.

The missile fell uselessly. The she-beast reared, spitting, haunches quivering, and for the first time he saw his master's resolve falter. Simons gawped with terror and his mouth gaped, his aspect no longer commanding. He dropped the spade onto his sandalled toe and winced. The creature stood inches before him, and he met its mesmerising stare. It sniffed, glancing at the seeping wound on his foot, smelling his blood, sensing his fear. It pinned him to the trunk, its lips puffing misty breaths of green as they closed on his ….

But then, it turned its head towards Thomas, suddenly aware of his presence.

It approached, releasing its grip of its flailing victim's throat. He slumped and slid down the bole of the yew. Thomas froze, entranced by its – *her* eyes – pools of shimmering hues, alternating from purple to aquamarine, with pupils wide and seducing. Her mien – her *bearing* – he recognised. She was small, wiry and agile, half starved, and with fingers tapering to talons replacing the nails. They were a darker shade of green than the flesh of her naked body, the skin of which appeared wizened and mummified; her breasts weighted by aquatic crustaceans clinging to the teats. Thin, black, straggly hair sprouted from her scalp, some strands reaching as far as her shoulders. Algae and mud slime slithered from her face and limbs.

Her pupils, too large for her hollowed cheeks, no longer glimmered. Her blackened teeth grinned in a grotesque parody of recognition and love, and made his spine ice up. It *was* the girl and she recognised him, but with an evil mockery of her pleading and innocence.

The water sprite reverted her attention to his master, slumped and helpless against the tree. She squatted over him akin to a hawk devouring its prey, and her bony, clawed phalanxes tore the habit from his chest and gripped the flesh covering his heart. The writhing pincers began to squeeze. His eyes and mouth stretched as his agonised moans morphed to guttural burbling.

Thomas shook his head in order to banish any sentiment. '*Foolish boy*' his master had said in his wisdom. He grasped the fallen spade and bashed the back of the blade onto the sprite's spine. The bones snapped, the body contorted, and she cried with a reedy shrill, her body suspended limp in the air. She fell backwards, breasts and hollow stomach exposed to him. For a moment he saw her face again – her *true* face, displaying tears of love and despair – but he shut his eyes and spun the handle of the spade in his fingers. With a heavy blow, he severed the head with the tip of the blade, and a fountain of oily, black blood spurted onto him; the putrid stench causing him to retch. The head rolled away, dropping into an open grave. The torso twitched and writhed, as if still living – an act of Beelzebub, he was certain – before it lurched and disappeared into the rushes.

Thomas made the sign of the cross, thankful for his safe deliverance, but also because the twitching, writhing form was hidden from his sight.

Father Simons had been spared. He'd recovered his staff and had propped himself against the base of the trunk. He rubbed his throat and chest, wheezing. Slowly his wide-eyed stare receded.

"Is she … is *it* truly dead now, Father?"

Simons raised a trembling finger and pointed at the pit. The severed head with the rolled back pupils and the blackened protruding tongue had ceased twitching. "I think so, my boy, though I'm not entirely sure … I don't know *everything!*"

Thomas supported him as he rose, helping him take the weight off his blooded foot, while his stricken master issued his instructions between gritted teeth and laboured breaths: "Find the gravediggers and tell them to burn its carcass to a crisp … then instruct them to reconstitute the earth … now though, help me back to the priory."

***

That night, Thomas lay on his hammock in the dormitory listening to the whine of a blowing gale. Shadows from a bough cast a dancing silhouette through a tiny window on the opposite wall, and the euphony of the brothers' chant at Vigil drifted in the ether pervading the hallowed chambers of the monastery. It lulled him. Owing to his exertions, the Prior had excused him from attending, and his master lay resting in the infirmary.

But when the wind dropped - suddenly, and not through an act of The Lord - he knew he had to atone. The breeze mimicked a sigh - a sigh like that of the girl. The clouds had lifted and a pale moon shone.

He thought of her waiting for him by the yew and her tender look of submission, love and gratitude.

… And of the heathens at the circle of megaliths with their torches of flame, and of the purity of the virgins' sacrifice as their flesh glistening wet by the heat, smouldered, charred and burned.

… our flesh's'truest form.

He wept.

The following day he made his excuses and returned to the chapel with bread. Rooks still cawed and sap still bled from the crust of the yew. A desperate feeling of hope had formed inside him.

She stood within the shadow of the dark leafy yew; an elfin figure in the shawl of a pauper. Her aspect and colours made it appear as though she had emerged from the russet red bark itself.

Father Simons was wrong; she was no water sprite.

As she took the hamper from him, a tear of devotion seeped from her moistened eye, and with her slender fingers she stroked his cheek. She pulled him to her and placed a loving palm on his breast, causing his heart to beat fast and his blood to pump.

Not fingers but talons.

Then she began to squeeze ….

Cragside, Rothbury, Northumberland
I remember approaching Cragside after a long and tiring walk, looking up and gazing in awe at the building's setting against the backdrop of a deep blue sky and dazzling sun. The house looked as rugged as the rocky crags and conifers it rises from.

A story based on lonely walks, bad dreams, creeping anxiety and blood-red sunsets.

Beside Me

It is hard to pinpoint the exact moment when I started to feel uneasy. I suppose it must have been when the sun began to lower in the sky, and when its rays shone so incredibly bright into our eyes … the point when it made its slow descent to the horizon, splashing gold amid the lengthening fingers of shadows that were creeping across the landscape. We had been walking all day and we were hot and perspiring. Our limbs ached and I for one felt tired, but contented, and I looked forward to a refreshing shower, a beer, a meal, and rest.

But there was a long way to go yet.

I could see the dirt track twisting along the narrow gorge ahead. It veered behind a rocky outcrop then plunged down a steep slope and out of sight. It re-appeared on the opposite side of the ravine as it tapered into the distance up the next rise, before disappearing into woodland. Beyond lay more slopes, hills and clumps of trees as the track headed out of the valley.

That's how it unfolded as the swollen orb of the golden sun came to rest at the exit point on the crest and blot my vision. *That, I knew was the way ahead, and the end of our journey.*

The intense glare must have made me avert my eyes and turn to my companion. She read my thoughts and answered my unspoken question.

"Yes, all we have to do is descend the slope, climb the next rise, and enter the woodland. Once we have passed through and reached the top of the hill yonder, we shall have arrived at our destination."

Her words seemed to come from inside my head, and I cannot recall turning and facing her, or uttering my words. But I'm certain she was there beside me.

We were deep within the ravine and the terrain rose steeply either side of us. Clusters of gorse and pine trees peppered both slopes, and beech and firs topped each summit, their silhouettes stark against a darkening azure sky. Way up there, the sun still shone brightly, but its dominion down here was waning – those creeping shadows all around us, closing in …

Yes … that's when I started to feel uneasy.

As we began the steep descent, the sun's rays hit me full on, blinding me. They danced and flickered, and my eyes shut in spasm. It was tortuous; I squinted and shielded them with my arm. I touched my companion's sleeve, and for a second, only for a second, I thought I saw her face.

… But just a fleeting glimpse before the dazzling rays blotted it out … leaving only an iris and pupil; large, translucent, expanding, contracting, and framed within a row of lush eyelashes. It watched me in the suffusing darkness.

"Soon … soon we will reach our destination." Her whispers flitted inside my head.

We entered a copse of alder and ash, their branches twisting above and enclosing us. I'm sure I could hear faint scurrying movements from within – unseen creatures of the dark preparing for their nocturnal wanderings. Each rustle, each cracking of a twig unnerved me – I sensed they were watching me … that is, watching *us*, I mean to say.

We cleared the copse, and re-entered the open, grateful for any final vestiges of light the sun would grant us. It was then that I realised that we weren't quite so alone. I could see the truck in the distance. The noise of the engine, and the grinding of the gears disturbed our solitude as it struggled to climb the next rise. We were gaining on it and I was unsure whether to be annoyed at this intrusion into our world, or be reassured that we were not the only travellers in this lonely spot.

It was carrying felled timber – loaded to the hilt – and the cause of its difficulties. It twisted and lurched until inevitably a wheel buckled over a protruding rock on the track. It stalled, and the rear of the truck skewed; thus, the logs started to spill. They bounced, splintered and scattered, the din echoing like thunder across the valley, but most had piled behind the lorry, now dead ahead of us. Our route was blocked.

"We'll never get beyond that …" I remember thinking those words.

My heart sank at the prospect of not completing our journey. It would indeed be a long, and very tiring hike back to where we had come from … wherever that was.

"We cannot go back" my companion seemed to say as, once again she read my thoughts. *"Ahead is our destination; there is no other way."* Her timbre was so reassuring; it compelled me, no, *willed* me, to obey… almost.

What a mess; logs were strewn everywhere. A man sprung from behind the far side of the truck. I jumped.

"Don't worry, pal, we'll soon have this lot shifted and we'll all be on our way again."

A surly, unshaven individual with muscles bursting from a checked shirt, and a sneering grin of crooked teeth, he raised his arm and clicked his fingers, his fixed gaze on me unwavering. "C'mon Aji, lad, look sharpish. We've got to clear this lot up so that the gentleman can pass."

A youth appeared, dressed in similar attire, his grin more playful and mischievous. He stole me a mocking glance, but his visage was also obscured by the evening shadows, save for his gleaming eyes and a toothy beam … and an earring that sparkled from a sunray. "OK, Boss."

As they laboured with the reloading of the logs,

more for the need to distract me from the interminable wait, I spoke:

"So where are you headed for?"

"Same destination as you," Boss replied. "Got to deliver these to Cragburn; the Master likes a good fire he does." He smiled slyly at the lad, then flicked his thumb towards the cabin of the truck. "We're taking the lass there too."

A young woman eyed us nervously from the rear window.

"You on your own then?" Boss enquired.

That puzzled me. I looked around for my companion. I knew she was there somewhere; hidden by the gloom, I supposed.

"Job's done, Boss." The lad brushed his hands together and leapt into the cabin.

Boss looked at me."You can come with us if you like; there's room for one more, and we're all travelling along the same road aren't we?" He may have been smirking, but it was difficult to tell in the fading light.

And … that's how your memory plays tricks on you. Why had he said "room for *one* more" when it was obvious that there were two of us? And I distinctly remember the youth's expression after his boss made that remark - his dark, studious brown irises weighing me up.

I climbed in, and Boss took his position at the wheel. Aji was already seated on the opposite side, so that the girl was sandwiched between us. She drew her limbs in, arms folded, and knees bunched to her chest. She glanced first at Aji, then to me, her aspect accusing, and with a downturned mouth. She was pale and pensive; I think she felt threatened.

I felt a little sorry for her, so once we were underway, and with a desire to break the ice and mask the silence, I enquired after her name.

"Poena."

That was strange. The name sounded pretty, and yet it seemed to unlock a distant, half-forgotten memory. It was odd, but it reminded me of my history studies as a student, and of the Romans and their deities. At last it clicked - Poena, the Roman goddess of punishment, and attendant to Nemesis, herself the goddess of vengeance and retribution. But my revelatory smile morphed to a frown; there was something else, something about that name.

"I'm a nurse. I take care of people. I have to get to Cragburn." She threw an accusatory stare at me; weighing me up. I lowered my eyes and the conversation died. Then she turned her face away, and gazed through the windscreen in silence; her body inert.

There was nothing left but to catch the dying sun across the landscape, and watch the splashes of gold flicker over their faces; momentary flares upon vacant expressions. That, and listen to the grinding protest of the motor as we endured the slow ascent up the next rise and left the ravine.

Oh, now I remember; my companion *was* still with me. I know this, because her hand held mine. I felt it. Besides, I recall one of the last of the sun's rays forming a bright, translucent pool on her slender palm and making it gleam. I could see the bones – a trick of the light, I guessed – as it protruded from the sleeve of what must have been her black shawl … those long, thin, death-white fingers wrapped round my palm.

***

The sun was setting. The truck laboured up the rise. The ghostly outline of the approaching wood brooded against the murky sky. As we entered, the flame red beams were extinguished; doused like a candle, and it cast the world into dusk. No-one spoke, and the lurching motor rumbled on and on.

Then the girl – the inert form beside me – broke the ether. "Stop; please stop, I need to get out."

"Out of the question; we have to get to Cragburn," Boss said, his voice, determined.

"Stop, stop now, I need the toilet."

"But our master insists!". He gripped the wheel and clenched his teeth.

"You want I pee in the truck?"

He cursed, slammed the brake and the vehicle screeched to a halt. He cut the ignition.

"Let me out please," she asserted, her tone miserable and insistent.

With a reluctant nod from the driver, Aji opened and leapt from his door. He let her pass and she bounded over to the nearby wall of trees and disappeared into the twilight.

We sat in silence. The sounds of the approaching

night soon began to play on my senses – the rustling of leaves on the woodland floor, the splinter of twigs, and the pitter-patter of myriad nocturnal creatures' restless stirrings. Each sound startled me and I cast nervous glances this way and that.

"Badgers, maybe foxes, or roe deer," my companion seemed to say to me, her whispers soothing and reassuring.

I alighted from the cabin – I needed to stretch my legs – and Boss followed. I peered into the canopy of pines – an endless tunnel, tapering to infinity in both directions – and the curtain of tree trunks either side of us; they walled us in like guarding sentinels. And I thought how odd this was – wasn't this supposed to be a mere copse; a clump of ash and alder on the track by the ridge?

The rustling noises intensified; things were moving, stirring – heard, but not seen. The waiting was interminable.

"She's not coming back, Boss." Aji's pupils glinted alertly, his perpetual toothy grin clear and animate in the grey.

Boss rubbed his stubbly chin and stared into the woods.

"Shall I go fetch her?" the youth asked.

Again no answer, and so after a pause, Aji sprinted off in the direction she'd fled.

Something was wrong, quite wrong; our afternoon adventure had long since vanished, and things were not making any sense at all; I felt quite afraid.

It was getting dark, so dark, and I could no longer determine the features of the driver – Boss – as he stood with his back to me, gazing at the road ahead, rubbing his chin, facing infinity. He could attack us at any moment. I feared for my – *our* – safety, for I knew my companion remained close to me because I glimpsed her form from the corner of my eye – a black shroud and cowl. But it is so unnerving to think that I cannot recall talking to, or looking at her directly, and yet I was certain that she was beside me … or within me … kind of ….

A horrible, piercing scream of such utter pitch and despair assaulted my ears. I jumped for the second time. It echoed around the woods and caused a commotion of fluttering avian wings and panic-stricken creatures scurrying in every direction. I fell to my knees, cowering, and covered my head with my hands.

"What the *hell* was that?"

"The lad's right; she ain't coming back, and that's a fact," Boss nodded, still rubbing his chin and staring into the void.

With a sudden about turn, he retreated to the truck. "And he ain't either. C'mon, we have an appointment at Cragburn."

We followed him and clambered in … my companion and I.

And she whispered to me,*"Do not worry … as soon as we are out of the woods, beyond the valley, and at the top of the rise, we will have arrived at our destination."*

I would have yielded to her soothing, repetitive mantra, but for a second howl that stabbed the air. It came from the woods, only nearer, and I could almost feel its hollow echo travel through the ether and hit my eardrums. Whoever it was desperately needed our help.

Boss fired the ignition, but I grabbed his wrist. I caught a movement in the wing mirror, and, within the eerie red glow of the tail-lights, I saw a figure running towards us. It was the girl, Poena. She stumbled in her desperation, but picked herself up again. My grip on him tightened and his eyes flared as he bared his crooked teeth.

But I was determined. "We've got to give her a chance!"

Then she was upon us. When I opened the cabin door, I'm sure I heard the lamenting wails of other, more distant cries, but they were muffled in the twilight and trees. She was breathless and staggering as I hauled her into the cabin beside me, and with a screech of the wheels, the truck surged forwards. She heard the voices too, because she glanced behind her.

Our eyes met, and I remember thinking that her mien was not that of terror; it was furtive – a look of guilt, I'd say – and that was strange considering her clothes were torn and muddy, her hair was bedraggled, and her skirt and top were spattered with blood.

Her eyes were accusing, and glowered at me from out of her mud stained face.

"He's dead … or at least he soon will be, after they've finished tormenting him, judging, and sentencing him."

"They? What on earth are you talking about?"

"He ... *you*, should have let me go; let me return."

A third cry – the youth's final, dying howl, far-off now – rang out as we moved on.

She resumed her posture: shoulders hunched, knees drawn up and staring pensively at the road ahead. And we listened to the rumble and drone of the labouring motor in the repressive quietude.

Still ...

My unseen, unheard companion stayed with me. I know this, for I could hear her breath on my ear, and feel its icy caress on my nape.

***

And time did not seem to follow its normal rules either. One moment we were engulfed by the impenetrable wall of trees, with its concealment of invisible sounds and horrors, and peering anxiously at the pinprick of light in the distance, the light at the end of the tunnel ... the next we were out on the open trackway, and gazing at the setting sun at its very moment of death. The swollen orb was sinking below the skyline; it spread its last tendrils of fire across the cliffs and valleys in a blaze of orange, and caught the driver's vacant, glazed expression.

We pulled up on the verge of the dirt track and stepped from the truck – it seemed the right thing to do.

Behind us, far below, lay the thick canopy of pine and firs we had journeyed through, and beyond that, the gorge where we had first met our fellow travellers. I watched it all turn from blood-red to ash. Ahead of us, stretched a narrow winding path, which meandered through a rough and rising landscape of jagged rocks and boulders that were peppered with heathers of purple, and ferns of green.

Cragburn! At least I knew where I was … something was beginning to dawn on me.

The climb would be arduous.

My eyes traced the path as it wound its way up the steep rise to the house at the summit – to the Victorian villa with its imposing mock Norman crenellated towers on either side. They frightened me.

As a boy, I had been taken there to convalesce after my illness, and I started to think about that far-off, awful day when I arrived at the foot of the rise – the exact point where I stood now. I had not wanted to go there, and worse, I could sense the malignance that lurked inside, the minute I'd set eyes on the house.

I remember the nurse, or 'Nanny' as I had always called her, grasping my hand and yanking at my arm as we began our slow ascent. I pleaded with her not to take me, but as her impatience grew, she scolded me. "Don't be silly, don't be silly; you need to be firm …."

And I remember how, when we had almost reached the summit, she paused for breath. The edifice loomed over us from above the rocks, heather and ferns. Its gleaming stonework set against an azure sky, and its linear Victorian bay windows – its eyes – glistened in the sunlight. It resembled a visage judging and condemning me, and underneath the eaves, the diamond shape window of the attic room, jutted from walls of dark wooden beams and white plaster. It was as if an eccentric architect, driven to insanity, had gotten hold of an Elizabethan manor house and planted it, right there on the roof, abutting it with a Norman keep.

I kept thinking that there would be an ogre or monster – a demon – lurking within a black void that must surely exist beyond the door, and once we crossed the threshold, we'd be doomed for certain. I could not understand why she was being so cruel. Why was she doing this to me? I yearned for the familiar, warm, safe feeling I got when I nestled close to her hip and thigh, or the feel of her starched tunic taut across her bosom.

The memory of her pointing to the attic room and telling me that it would be *my* room lingers. It's when I snatched myself free and retreated down the path – I had to get away from there. I can still hear her calling me back, and her footsteps gaining on me. That's when it happened. She must have lost her footing on the uneven ground and tripped, because I heard a sudden shriek, and a muffled thud. I stopped and turned. She had fallen on to her back, and was straddling the sharp, prickly thorns of heather that grew so close to the precipitous slope beside the path, and she bore a contorted, agonised expression.

"Help me, I've twisted my ankle, I can't move it … the pain."

I walked over, and just stared at her. The heather and thorns had scratched her face and specks of blood soiled her white tunic. She was attempting to grab ahold of a branch by the path. I have flashbacks of her writhing, blooded fingers … and how her grip was too feeble. I hated her now. Why was she leaving me here, all alone? I stamped on her hand in a fit of rage. Her eyes stretched, her mouth gaped and she made a funny, winded noise. She jerked backwards and tumbled down the incline. I'll never forget her scream, and how it stopped abruptly as she hit the first boulder with a sickening cracking of her bones. It sent her spiralling in a different direction, and she plummeted from a sheer drop. I heard her impact the ground with a faint thud. She lay on a rocky outcrop hidden in a bed of shrubs, her limbs splayed and her neck bent horribly. I still suffer awful visions of her agonised, frozen stare looking up at me. It gave me nightmares for many years to come.

I was right about the architect. I later discovered that the house had been built by a wealthy Victorian engineer and inventor who, upon moving into the abode, became increasingly eccentric, to the point of insanity. Stories abound of course, but it is said that something, perhaps an evil spirit, dwells on that hill, and got to him. He became a recluse, and after he died, on searching the dwelling, the bodies of his wife, daughter and maid were discovered. All were murdered - drowned, stabbed or poisoned - and, it seems, with 'unholy rituals' (as contemporary accounts described it) performed on the bodies. The body of the wife, the last to die, had been laid out on a huge funeral pyre of logs in the rear courtyard prior to cremation; a bizarre attempt to copy an Iron Age funeral wake. The shaman priests had practised similar rituals on the hill and surrounding area two thousand years ago, according to archaeologists. Locals believe that the spirits of the tribe's ancestors roam the landscape, and take possession of the creatures that dwell there. The mountains, gorges, valleys and woods are 'alive' with malignant spirits, all taking the form of the animals residing within. They had also possessed the inventor, compelling him to continue with their gruesome ways. But something prevented him from completing the task – they say his heart gave out, and he collapsed dead by his wife's feet. When they were eventually found, the cadavers were substantially decomposed, but, according to the coroner, the look of terror on both remained frozen and vivid.

"No need for a driver now; we make our way on foot."

The voice of Poena broke my macabre reminiscences. She moved towards the driver. The rough, burly man stood trance-like on a nearby crag with his glazed eyes glistening in the reddening sunset. Slowly, reluctantly, he turned his head and faced her. It's odd but … she suddenly had dominion over him.

She pressed her hand on his shoulder, and he began to quiver and tremble, his gaze fixed on her death stare. His eyes rolled up, his mouth opened, but he emitted no cry. Then his knees buckled, and he sank to the ground.

She stared down at him; his strength was ebbing and blood trickled from his lolling tongue, and I could not tear myself away from her cold, accusing expression. I felt no compassion for the man, who for so long had subjugated the girl; he seemed pathetic and powerless and was receiving his just deserts. And when I looked down at the crouching figure again, he was gone -vanished without trace.

Her demeanour was terrible, so resentful and judgemental. Whatever the man and the youth had done to her in the past I shall never know, but she had despatched them with such utter ruthlessness. But what had been *my* crime? She turned to me as if to answer, and I followed her pointing finger towards the house at the summit.

"Time to make the journey again," she said.

"To make the final leg of the journey," whispered my companion, still beside me and within me.

The sun had finally set, and everything was cast in twilight.

She commenced the slow climb up the winding path, and I attended obediently, along with my unseen companion. The path twisted and wound between the rocks and shrubs, and she never tired. I stayed close to her but the steepening incline caused me to falter as the sharp, unforgiving thorns brushed and clawed at my clothes and skin.

But I *had* to stay close to her … close to her hips, and sense the rustle of her skirts brushing my cheek and feel protected next to her broad, robust body. I was drawn to the curves, and longed for the warm, safe feeling I loved when I walked beside her; a feeling I used to get a long time ago … as a boy.

And then I realised who she was.

My nurse.

Nanny.

She had barely reached eighteen on that fateful day when she had plunged to her death – the day I killed her – and that it is why, all these years later, as a grown man, I had not recognised her. Back there, in the woods and gorge, she appeared as a young woman, a mere slip of a girl.

Of course … Poena, the attendant to Nemesis; goddess of vengeance and retribution, and of just resentment and anger; the distributor of fortune in due proportion to each man according to his deserts – the men in the truck, and the recluse who lived in that awful abode. Now it was my turn, this was *my* nemesis.

She stopped at the very spot where I had broken free last time, crouched and faced me. I couldn't discern her expression in the dusk, but I could hear her weeping. They were tears of betrayal and hurt – but not vengeance.

The house loomed behind her – a brooding, dark outline against the grey sky with its Gothic towers and its large bay windows watching me like soulless eyes.

I knew I had to make the choice. And so it was *my* turn to sink to my knees. I looked up at her, clutched at her skirts and shut my eyes, as before.

"Do we enter the house, or not?" asked my companion.

"I can't … there's something ancient, something evil that dwells in there … the attic … behind the windows … the inventor who went mad, the women who died … ghosts, demons …yes, demons …. I can't …."

I opened my eyes to face Nanny again, but she wasn't there. I saw her spread-eagled far below on a crag down the incline, the life force seeping from her in an expanding pool. Her body and blood gleamed bright, as though the sun had never set and was casting its light on her lifeless form; a shining angel embroidered on vermilion velvet.

A pale, skeletal hand touched mine. I turned to my companion, still shrouded in her black, baggy shawl, the cowl hiding her from me.

"So be it.

"But you know that we all have to make this final journey… to face our demons. And you have failed once more. Now … we make the journey again …."

I peered into her cowl but it slipped away, and, through the gloom, her death-white skull with the hollow eye-sockets, grinned back at me. The icy sigh of her breath enveloped me.

***

… There was a long way to go yet.

I could see the dirt track twisting along the narrow gorge ahead. It veered behind a rocky outcrop then plunged down a steep slope and out of sight. It re-appeared on the opposite side of the ravine as it tapered into the distance up the next rise, before disappearing into woodland. Beyond lay more slopes, hills and clumps of trees as the track headed out of the valley.

"Soon … soon we shall arrive at our destination," my companion seemed to say within me and beside me.

That, I knew, was the way ahead, and the end of our journey ….

Binham Priory, Norfolk

A tale set in a ruined priory; the original nave is still used as a parish church.

Rumours abound of a secret underground passage that leads to Little Walsingham, and the ghost of a monk in black robes that resides nearby.

A fiddler and his dog once set out to explore it, playing a tune as he went so that people above ground could follow on the surface. Suddenly the music stopped (below what later became known as 'Fiddler's Hill') and although the hound emerged shivering in terror, the tunesmith was never seen again. It is believed that he had been carried off by a figure in black.

Later, upon excavating a round barrow at the same spot, three skeletons, including a female and a dog, were unearthed.

The Custodian

The remains of the lofty Norman archway of the decaying gatehouse neatly framed the view of the south facing wall of the priory church. Harry contemplated its grandeur as he sat in the car, the engine idling. Then, he carefully drove through and pulled up.

As he stepped from the car, a sunray pierced the rain clouds and illuminated the magnificent wall of flint and red brick. It sparkled in the golden light like sea salt on shingle.

A sense of relief washed over him. This place, so familiar from childhood, was to be his home for the next few months. He needed no persuading in accepting the job of custodian - an overseer - while the workmen and craftsmen preserved the ruins in preparation for the visitors who would undoubtedly return next spring.

He passed through the wrought-iron gate and bound up the slope so as to gain a better view of the architecture from the eastern side. But the sunray extinguished and the chill interrupted; he looked at his boots embedded in the rain soaked grass and shuddered.

The priory church, the only building still intact, stood resplendent, overlooking the crumbling monastic walls, and the foundations of cloisters, dormitories and work rooms that sprawled and disfigured its east and north aspects. He remembered standing there long ago with his school chum Buckley on that very same spot. Then of course the sun always shone, and it was always summer. Then, the church had gleamed white, with its wide buttresses standing squat against the eastern wall like the huge skeletal remains of a dinosaur lying forever still in the shallow valley; its carcass surrounded by shattered masonry resembling the husks and shells and the leftovers of its carnivorous meal. Such wild imaginings had fed the two boys' appetite for adventure.

With the passing of days they'd grown up, lost touch and left their boyhood capers far behind them. Then came that fateful day at Breckham-Staithe last year …

That day on the salt marshes shook him more than he cared to admit, especially after that subsequent business with Annie. But his luck changed. Quite by chance he discovered Buckley was working in the area. He forgot his torment, and buried himself in the comfort of the past. Buckley, it seemed, was overseeing the archaeological and historical discoveries at the nearby priory. Indeed, it was on Buckley's insistence that he succeed him in the role of custodian, and so here he was!

His heart sang, and as he ambled among, the ruins the sunray reappeared, and the dripping dew glistened.

Of course … there was another matter that needed resolving but that would have to wait.

Each arch, corbel, window frame and turning of a corner, reminded him of their reunion last year. He'd spotted Buckley from the perimeter wall of the priory directing operations with his typical assertive, articulate trait. As Buckley shook him firmly by the hand, he looked just as he imagined he would when they had come of age – tweed jacket and bow tie and with a mop of floppy hair crowning his broad forehead. He was every inch a scholar from a bygone era; a natural leader, enthused by whatever new and eccentric enterprise he'd immersed himself in.

"Funny how the place still strikes a chord with us after all this time," he said as he slapped Harry on the back during their nostalgic tour of the ruins. "Boyhood adventures and imagination and so forth.

Speaking of which, do you remember our talk of a secret tunnel that supposedly leads from here to the salt marshes half a mile or so north of here?"

"And the pot of gold that lies therein?" Harry beamed.

Buckley's eyes widened conspiratorially, "Well, I'm on to it."

He had led him into a small chamber behind the north wall of the church, which, choked with invading briar and bramble, was open to the elements and permanently in shade. A misshapen ash tree grew in the corner, its boughs and twigs sprawled as though they had been picking away at the broken flint walls when no-one was looking.

"I remember this; this was our den."

"Yes," Buckley affirmed in his confident, precise manner. "It's the apse of a much earlier church than the one we see today; Saxon, I think, and so an older building. It's where the tunnel starts, I'm certain of it."

Buckley gripped the lapel on his tweed jacket between his finger and thumb, smoothed his thick mop of hair, and his eyes narrowed studiously.

"Our fabled passageway runs from the south transept from the church's interior, on the other side of this wall."

And the sun lit up his face, just as it had from the far-off days of boyhood.

A sudden chill in the damp air caused Harry to break from his reminiscing; more rain clouds were threatening. He glanced at his sodden boots and returned to the iron gate, retreating to the shelter of the church's south facing door.

The warmth and calm inside welcomed him. Still used by the local parishioners, the church was closed for the winter and the duration of the renovation. The workmen had already departed for the day but had installed a temporary generator, and its low hum within the stillness lulled him; that and the smell of polished pews and an inviting array of display cases. The rows of archaeological relics - weathered sculpted masonry of gargoyles and long dead clerics - glimmered eerily in the dingy, tungsten gloom, their faces hidden in shadow … except for the eyes, which seemed curiously alive. Somehow, it added to the calming serenity of his surrounds. Scattered among them were medieval parchments of religious learning, the gaudy colours of the manuscripts were illuminated by the glow.

The peace and spiritual tranquillity that encompassed him would help banish thoughts of Annie.

A flight of steps rose from the side of the aisle up onto a short balcony. From there, an arched door with a low stone lintel led to a small room that was home to the prior in medieval times. A bunk, a chest of drawers and a writing desk (upon which rested a laptop and phone),was all that furnished the room, apart from a wash basin and a stove. Basic but cosy; his home for the coming months. It was all he needed and he relished his forthcoming stay there during the winter. Should he require any further provisions, or, perish the thought, human company, he could always seek assistance from the nearby village.

An ornate latticed window overlooked the cloister ruins, the walls of which remained intact, although the roof no longer existed. It provided a pleasing view.

He unpacked his case. A momentary flicker of the light and the snuffing out of the generator's low hum brought a heavy silence and compelled him to pause, his thoughts weighing on him. He relished his solitude, but … what *did* happen to Buckley?

The light came on again.

Following their renewed acquaintance last summer, Buckley's enthusiasm over the renovations, and his search for the mythical lost passageway and treasure, meant that he'd kept in touch via frequent emails and phone calls.

"Success! Carstairs, I've done it; the final clue, I've solved the riddle. I'll send you a copy of my thesis later." – Buckley's voicemail – his last.

He'd vanished into thin air, and hadn't been in touch since.

Buckley's patron was also baffled; as much in the dark as Harry was, and especially as to his curious instruction for Harry to succeed him as custodian. But such was Buckley's academic prestige that they agreed, no questions asked – and besides, they had deadlines to meet and reputations to keep.

So now this was Harry's domain; his responsibility; his passion, his *obsession*. The hard work having being done, all he had to do was oversee the remaining repairs – appoint personnel, arrange supplies and logistics and so on – and to make sure the place was ready for summer.

That, and to find Buckley…

Of course, there was another reason he was here, one that he hardly dare admit to himself. Deep down, he was hoping that Annie would come. He waited for her in dreadful anticipation, and yet … the prospect of her failure to arrive was too awful to contemplate.

After all, there were issues that needed resolving ….

***

That night he dreamed.

The nights were drawing in, and, after a toasted cheese supper and a tot or two of sleep inducing whisky, he'd retired early. Wind driven rain pattered against the latticed window and the darkness from outside encroached on him.

Ever since that fateful day on the salt marshes, he had learned to control his dreams. He'd lie on his back, breathe slowly and deeply, and they would begin. He would relive that late September afternoon and she would return ….

He had left the coastline pathway, weary, but exhilarated and wandered across the vast carpet of green, mossy sponge that stretched to the distant shoreline. The samphire felt rubbery and sturdy beneath his feet. The sun was bright; its beams lighting the expanse of greens, reds and browns with a golden sheen as far as the eye could see. Only a thin strip of yellow and azure – the sand and sea on the horizon – separated this alien world from the vast, pale blue sky. Wisps of white cirrus clouds drifted high above like sailing vessels in an ocean sky.

The strip of sand and sea was his goal, simply because it was there. He marvelled at the vista in awe – he could see why people got lost out there; how easy it was to get disorientated and to lose one's bearings. And he was the only soul for miles around.

But the warming sun and the sound of the gulls' screeches lulled him. He could always follow the line of the sewer pipe if *he* got lost. It led from inland, and out to sea – the pipe would be his landmark; his compass.

Eventually the forest of weed thinned and gave way to sand flats. The sigh of the ocean grew to a roar and the spray glistened as he drew nearer to its edge. The strand turned compact and wet and stuck to his boots, and the eddying tide churned it into great swathes of gloopy brown clumps, which dried out then wetted again. Tell-tale signs of mud worms pockmarked its smoothened surface. Vast, clear pools of brine appeared, the surface water rippling and sparkling in the bright. Sand particles swirled in the wind, striking him in accord with the myriads of tiny, attacking sand flies, and he noticed how the boil of the incoming tide had turned against him; it roared like an angry lion. Strange how Nature's mood could alter so quickly, and in the time it took for a spitting fleck of salt-spray to blind him.

He should be heading back.

If he stayed close to the pipeline, he would maintain his bearings.

He halted for a moment; something caught his eye – a shimmering speck on the open flats. A figure, black, inert and watching as though aware of his presence; its face a distant blur, but unnerving. Its hair flapped in the breeze; a woman maybe, but too far-off to tell.

The roll of the surf was deafening and would soon be upon him. Nevertheless, if someone else had ventured this far into the wilderness, they'd help each other and find a way back.

He retraced his steps alongside the pipeline, glancing over his shoulder and expecting her to follow, but instead the figure receded, and when he looked again, she'd vanished. How was that so? There was no place to hide in the open expanse, but he was quite alone.

When he gazed ahead once more, the pipe had also disappeared. True, the gorse and weeds thickened as he headed inland, covering the ground beneath him, but surely it should still be visible … nearby … somewhere.

Low-lying cloud had appeared and patches of darkness blotched the vista, confounding his sense of unease. They blotted the sun, and the wind blew cold. The sunlit marshlands shed their golden colours and grew dull and sullen.

Best to use his instincts and take short-cuts. He could see drier patches of sand dunes beyond the samphire and gorse. He stepped into the wetted scrub and soon made his way to the firmer terrain - done! But then the pathway narrowed, gradually petering out, and he was back in the undergrowth and unsure of his footing. He re-entered the weed and successfully reached higher ground, but that also proved to be a dead-end. He repeated the process, several times. The dry land and the coast path seemed no nearer.

With all his exertions he hadn't noticed how the rumble of the tide had dampened to muffled huffs and sighs.

He looked behind him. Worry turned to alarm. The band of yellow and azure had been smothered by a veil of greyness.

Sea mist!

It was rolling in at an incredible speed and would soon engulf him. He had no choice but to hasten - keep going and hope for the best. Surely, the nearer he got, the firmer and more secure the terrain underfoot would become.

Disaster struck - a sudden jarring of the spine, and down he went. He'd lost his footing, and a sharp pain seared through his ankle. He cursed at his own clumsiness. His boot stuck fast in the quicksand. He tugged and he tugged, until eventually, his foot prised free. But the spasms in his ankle were excruciating. How could he have been so complacent, so … *stupid*?

The sea mist enveloped him, twisting grey, mimicking a shoal of ghostly eels. It felt cold and clammy against his skin. But at least the freezing squelch of water in his boot numbed the pain. He picked himself up. Yes… he could still walk, albeit slowly; more of a hobble. Just keep moving forward – he was sure he was headed in the right direction …

The mist carried an eerie silence.

A voice shrieked from somewhere out in the murk.

A woman's cry, hollow and shrill.

Alarm turned to panic.

But if he panicked, he knew he was done for. After a dreadful pause, her bawl pierced the air twice … three times.

Was she in difficulty? Or was she calling to guide him? Impossible to tell.

He limped forward. Somehow the samphire and gorse thinned, the pathways opened up, and the brooding outline of trees lining the coast path appeared in the fog.

The terrible cries of the woman, wherever she was – ahead or behind him – trailed off. A sense of dread instilled him. If she remained there, trapped in the mist and at the mercy of the tides ….

He'd made it to the coast path. Exhausted now, he rested under the shelter of a nearby bush. There was still some coffee left in his thermos – that would help to revive him. Once he had gathered his wits, he would retrace his steps the mile or so down the track, then catch the coast bus to the village of Breckham-Staithe, the location of his digs, and seek help.

He'd barely travelled halfway along this, the

final wearisome part of his journey when the awful feeling that he was not alone returned to plague him.

He paused, and in the distance he saw the dark figure of the woman watching him … she'd survived. Her purposeful strides told him she was pursuing him. There was something about her gait; malevolence, scorn, hatred, something …

If he continued at his slow, shuffling pace, she would be upon him. He pressed onward, defying the pain from his injured ankle and summoning the last of his adrenalin.

She was gaining on him. He glanced over his shoulder again and again, each time she'd drawn closer, her hair bouncing and hiding her face, just a grey fuzzy disc. She wore long black skirts, and not a coat, he was certain of that, and seemed laden by a heavy wicker basket – its impediment may prove his salvation. He needed to get away from her, and he stopped looking round in case she sensed his trepidation … but she *would* catch him.

The steeply rising embankment on the pathway's leeward side – facing inland – rose to a ridge topped by trees that ran parallel to the track. When he dared another glimpse, she had vanished. He halted, and searched in all directions. Nothing save for his laboured breathing and the curlews' lament broke the stillness of the thickening sea mist; the silence fed on his fear.

She must have reached the break in the embankment he'd just passed. The rise led to the copse above him on the slope … so she *could* be alongside him, and spying on him, hidden amongst the trees. He noticed their leaves trembling from movements within ....

Tiny phuts upon the soft sand; raindrops forming in the mist.

No ... the patter of rain on the latticed window pane.

He awoke with a start, opening his eyes and staring into the surrounding darkness.

Only a dream - thinking about Annie too much. Why he always dreamed about that awful experience, he wasn't sure. He almost wished she'd catch up with him, rather than having to relive the ordeal over and over, so that he could, at last, resolve matters. It was, as he told himself many times, unfinished business.

***

Most of the following day was wasted while workmen tinkered unsuccessfully with the faulty generator. Inevitably its droning hum ceased abruptly with a crackling buzz and bang; the lights went out, and rendered almost everything inoperable.

Then there was another setback.

"The vaulted ceiling in the crypt is unsafe," the foreman said to him as he took off his helmet and wiped his brow. "We were clearing away the broken masonry at the back, when I noticed the deep fissures in the supporting pilasters. That'll mean getting in another lot of specialists."

"How long a delay?"

"Tomorrow… maybe the day after, what with that and the generator. OK, I can get it going again – sort of – but there's nothing else we can do here today. Sure you'll be all right here on your own?"

"Hm … can't really leave the property unattended."

"Oh, we found this …" The foreman handed him a large and yellowed crumbling parchment. "Of course you're the expert and you'll no doubt need to get it authenticated and preserved, but I unearthed it near the sarcophagus in the corner. I think it's the original plan of the early church and apse … long since disappeared. If I didn't know better, I'd say someone's put it there deliberately."

"… And for the custodian to find." Harry said with a half-smile. He welcomed the prospect of his enforced solitude.

***

"A tunnel … *Buckley's* tunnel," Harry smiled to himself as he studied the parchment back in the Prior's room. He downed the contents of the whisky glass, just as the lights flickered and the generator resumed its buzzing and crackling again.

He cursed as he lit a candle and placed it on the windowsill, but doused the flame quickly when he sensed a movement across the darkened cloisters below. The generator grumbled to life again, and the radiance from the church aisle beneath him flooded the ruins.

There it was again; a movement, a figure

caught in the glare, staring up at him. For a moment, he'd hoped it was Annie ....

Instead, a man; his face hidden by a huge, broad brimmed hat. Something scampered around his feet, and yet he could hear no sound, even though the wind and rain had dropped.

A drunk on his way home from the pub, trespassing with a view to looting, no doubt. It was a good job he'd stayed. He vanished between the flickering of the lights below – he was uncertain of the exact moment – but it was before they extinguished for good. He lit the candle once more, hoping its glow would quash his encroaching fear. There had been talk of the grounds being haunted by the last prior, executed during the time of the Reformation, but he didn't look like a monk ...

His hair prickled on his nape.

***

He awoke to a strange noise. In his half sleeping, half waking state, he assumed it was the whistle of the wind, until he remembered that had died ages since. A flute echoed in the air, and from somewhere distant. He crossed to the window. The candle had also died, drowned in a pool of melted wax.

There – the man with the broad brimmed hat stood below, scarcely visible in the light of a pale, watery moon. To his mouth, he held a stick– a *flute* – the source of the playful melody ringing in his ears. The creature continued to dart around in a blur.

He dressed quickly, arming himself with a

knife by the stove, but when he returned to the window the figure had disappeared.

Not so the tune; it whirled in his mind, growing louder. After another fortifying whisky he descended into the aisle of the church. The melodic waves, strangely familiar, were mocking him. The intruder had breached the building, for sure.

His eyes turned towards the west transept, and to the flickering shadows in a recess cast by a solitary candle. Who had lit that?

There – he'd reappeared.

He recalled the passageway that led off from there, and down into the crypt. The heady effects of the whisky blotted out thoughts of the foreman's warning, "not safe"; ahead of him he saw his youthful self and Buckley, his chum, as they set off on their trail of adventure. He was, after all, on Buckley's trail.

Armed with a torch and the knife in his hand, he took the candlestick from the niche in the wall, and descended the stone steps leading to the crypt. The flute ceased abruptly, leaving the echoes of his footsteps on the stone. His eerie jester knew he was following. The feeble nimbus from the tiny flame in his hand trembled in accord with the beating of his heart.

A sudden icy draught blew the candle out and the tune started again, magnified by its echoes bouncing on the walls of the crypt. He fumbled for his torch as the pitch-black pressed on him, feeding on his rising terror.

The beam danced around the void, settling in

the corner where he expected to confront his mocking tormentor.

Nothing but dust, broken masonry and scuttling spiders in cobwebs; a forgotten entrance to a passage barred by fallen rubble and an ancient, rusty iron grill that probably led to above ground. He was sure he glimpsed the haunches of a small dog recede within when the tune faded into the night.

***

The damp, early morning mist chilled his bones, doing its utmost to deter him from his quest. He shivered and wiped the clinging rain from his face. He was rewarded by his discovery of a storm drain, partially hidden by the ash tree behind the north wall of the church. It was located at the exit point of the passage from the crypt – the very spot where Buckley was certain the supposed missing tunnel would begin. If he got down on all fours, he could just make out the rusted iron grill he noticed from the other side last night.

"Ahem!"

Harry scrambled to his feet, shocked at the sudden intrusion. The site foreman wore an incredulous expression, glaring at him as though he was unhinged.

Harry brushed himself down, feeling a warm flush of embarrassment. "Good morning. I er … think I may have found the source of the so-called missing tunnel."

"Shouldn't you be taking a bit more care of that?" The foreman gestured to the parchment crumpled in Harry's fist.

"Er …yes, yes, I will. If this is accurate, the tunnel leads out of the priory grounds and towards that hill over there, beyond the meadow."

"Aye, that would be Fiddler's Hill as the locals call it."

"Fiddler's Hill eh? Mm … interesting."

"Anyway, just to tell you that the specialist mason won't be here until tomorrow, but in the meantime I'll get to work on the generator."

The foreman left him alone, shaking his head as he walked away.

OK so he thinks I'm nuts.

He lay prostrate on the soil, listening through the cover of the storm drain.

Well, there's nothing else to do today is there?

*Hah! I hear the berceuse of the merry tunesmith again; I **have** to see this through.*

He traced the route of the tunnel methodically, inching his way across the terrain and along the outline of the priory's robbed out walls and foundations, until he reached the perimeter. He scrambled over a fence and into the monks' old burial ground with the serenading of the flute rising from the turf below flooding his mind. It sang to him, the haunting melody egging him on. Another glance at the parchment confirmed the direction.

A weatherworn, lichen encrusted slab of sandstone lay at the centre of the burial ground. He took a handkerchief from his pocket and began to rub and scrape …

The outline of a crucifix … and an abbot or prior lying recumbent in his robes … of course! Hallowed earth; this is a tombstone … but it straddles the route of the tunnel.

As he pressed his ear to the rough stone, the flute sounded louder and more real. He heaved and clawed at the slab frantically, fearing he'd lose the playful melody, but it refused to budge. He rushed back to the priory, almost snatching a spade and crowbar from a startled workman.

He prised the sarcophagus lid from its base and the brittle sandstone fragmented and crumbled.

When he saw the falling steps, a crazed euphoria gripped him – he must hurry. The steps became drier and firmer as he descended underground … and away from daylight. Thank god he'd brought the torch.

They led to a walled passageway and a floor scattered with chippings of flint and rubble. The thought that it hadn't been walked upon for centuries – except that is for his ghostly, spellbinding minstrel – filled him with awe.

He edged into the tunnel and the encroaching darkness. The crunching of the stones beneath him echoed heavy, and the musty stink of mould irritated his nostrils. Brown, stained water dripped from the walls; it glistened in the torchlight.

The passage grew narrower, and eventually impassable; his elation evaporated in the miasma. He halted, undecided on his next course of action.

Should I turn back or find another route?

A movement at his feet, a brushing against his calf … the darting movements of a dog as it panted and whined. A fleeting glimpse before the tiny form bolted into the narrowing hole and disappeared as it searched for its master, whose ludic flute still continued to echo shrilly along the burrow.

He could still follow above ground ….

Once in the open again, he followed the course of the tunnel, past the cemetery and into the meadow towards Fiddler's Hill. Now he was on higher ground, and a breeze blew so that he had to strain his ears for the call of the flute. But he was certain he could hear it – it was inside his head.

He paused and glanced behind him and to the valley where the priory ruins nestled. Overcast clouds blanketing the rain sodden earth were creating a chill, and the low-lying mist was lingering. Then he took the last few strides towards the hummock ahead on the crest of Fiddler's Hill, his breath puffing, his heart thumping, but confounding the freezing air.

An indistinct, sentient shape emerged from out of the valley's blanket of fog – he saw it from the corner of his eye.

He swore he could hear her cries carried by the wind. He knew all along she would return.

He thought about his last ever meeting with Buckley, and his reaction when he told him of his encounter with her on the day he lost his way on the salt marshes:

Buckley had admonished him. "You were lucky. They call her Annie, though I'm not sure that's her real name. She was a cockle gatherer, lost and drowned somewhere out there amidst the quicksands and incoming tides. They say you can hear her cries when the fog descends, and she'll follow you to the shore if she spots you …"

He leaned forward, his wide eyes and round face looming. "Yes … you were lucky for if you happen to catch her expression, you'll be mesmerised by just how serene she appears … it's the resigned look of the drowned when the swirling water finally gives up its victim. A glint, the radiance of gold, is said to form in her eyes … a reflection of the treasure she's condemned to guard over for eternity."

"Treasure?"

He remembered how Buckley dismissed the word with a wave of his palm. "Either that, or you'll see something so ugly, so hideous …"

Unfinished business with Annie.

Harry watched transfixed as she ascended the grassy slope towards him. The melodious harmonies of the flute calmed him, but it suddenly stopped dead, halted by a momentary gust of wind. Then, a fretful whine … the unmistakeable cry of a frightened, whimpering hound. It tore out of the bramble beside the mound, terror-stricken, and scampered down the hill. It vanished in an unnatural blur.

He had no time to react; he wouldn't escape her this time. Another unearthly 'whoosh' hit him cold on the skin. He gasped. The black robed form was upon him and its limbs reached out and embraced him, its body as cold as ice. Its face, a grey, oval, featureless patch, brushed against his cheek. That's all he *could* see – nothing but putrid slime where her eyes should be, and rotting seaweed swaying from her blackened slit of a mouth. The stench of her breath assaulted him as her lips pressed upon his and sucked his breath away. As she crushed him, the gurgling rush and bitter taste of ice-cold salt water filled his nostrils and throat; it caused him to trip and fall into blackness and oblivion.

***

It wasn't until the following spring, when he stood in the valley and gazed up at Fiddler's Hill outlined against a clear blue sky, that he achieved any kind of resolution over what happened to him. As the mechanical digger churned up the layers of earth of the Saxon barrow, he thought back to that chill autumn day when the workmen had found him. He must have tripped and cracked his head on the protruding stones of the structure beneath – the burial chamber – and he was determined to uncover its secrets now. He had to; he owed it to himself and to Buckley, of whom there was still no sign.

Gradually the stones were unearthed and surrendered their secrets, but the three human skeletons they uncovered on that single day bore no relation to the myths and mysteries of pre-conquest England and the ancient kingdom of Anglia.

The first, a male, lay with his phalanxes clasped round a stone casket containing riches of gold. The hoard of coins confirmed the mound as Saxon, and the resting place of a wealthy nobleman. But no royal bones from the Dark Ages awaited them; only Harry saw the broad brimmed hat, and the whistle beneath the skull, and the tiny dog's skeleton nestled beside the remains - before the sudden rush of air and light turned it all to dust. It confirmed the story told to him by the frequenters of the village pub: One night, nearly two hundred years ago, a traveller, fuelled by the intoxication of ale and wine, had bet his fellow drinkers that if he walked the secret passageway said to have been built by the monks from centuries past, it would lead to a pot of gold. His trusty dog would guide him and unearth the treasure. The others could follow on the surface, guided by the call of his flute as he played. They set out on that fog shrouded night, but when the playing suddenly stopped, nothing was seen of the traveller again, except for his faithful hound - a fleeting glimpse - as it fled down the hillside in terror.

But it was the second skeleton alongside that caused the stir. Its bones reflected bright as they glistened in the midday sun, and its withered flesh remained taut on the cheekbones. The clothes - a tweed jacket and bow-tie - and a pile of shock-white hair on the wizened scalp, shook Harry to the core. Its hand also reached for the pot of gold.

No more archaeology would be had there today, or for a while.

But the report described only two skeletons. Harry saw three.

He stood alone, long after the gaggle of officials had departed. He found himself drawn to the bones inside the long black skirts and hood crouched in the excavated chamber in the far corner, and cast in shadow by an overhanging bough. How could they not have noticed?

He knew by the lack of ridges above the eye-sockets that it was a female. Her macabre gait told him she was guarding the treasure; acting as custodian, but also as jailer and guardian against her unfortunate victims – the other two skeletons – one fresh, the other hundreds of years old. They sprawled at her feet.

A narrow tunnel led off the exposed chamber and headed underground in the direction of the salt marshes and sea. A floating swirl of mist lingered from just inside the dimness beyond the tunnel mouth. He caught the shadowy figure watching from within for less than a heartbeat. The ghost of Annie looked down upon its remains … he swore he saw it turn its head and stare at *him*. She was, he supposed, doomed to serve as an acolyte of the ancient spirit guardian of the treasure on Fiddler's Hill.

Either way, that was the last time he actually *saw* her, though he always felt she was close beside him.

Even so, Harry resolved never to set foot near Breckham-Staithe again. He also made sure that he never went out into the fog alone, or on such nights when a mist descended in the silent air. On such nights, he wouldn't dare look out of the window.

Minster Lovell Hall and Dovecote, Oxfordshire
Hidden behind a church and beside a sleepy, meandering river, are the ruins of a 15th century priory, a place of tranquillity, reflection and imagination. Two ghosts are said to haunt the area: A White lady roams the ruins, the spectre of a bride trapped in an oak chest after an ill-fated game of hide-and-seek, and that of Francis Lovell, a fugitive of the Crown, who locked himself in an underground chamber in order to avoid capture. However, his attendant, the holder of the key, and the only person who knew of his whereabouts, unexpectedly died. Lovell's remains were discovered centuries later when builders were renovating the hall.

Moving On

I often sit here by the riverbank and gaze at the priory ruins behind me. They lie hidden aside the village church, just a short walk along the pathway amongst the yews. On a hot summer's day, I'll wander amid the decrepitude - the remnants seem out of place on the manicured lawns - and I'm especially drawn to the tower, because it seems to brood among the rest of the buildings. I want to enter -I'm curious - but the crumbling steps are far too dangerous to climb. Instead, I make my way down the grassy slope, and sit by the river under the shade of the trees hanging over the bank. I like to dangle my bare feet in the cool darkness of the water, as it flows lazily down stream.

Amidst the still and humid air, I can hear the fish 'plop' as they rise to the surface for air and morsels, and, just like the duck with her clutch of chicks as she waddles by me and goes about her daily business of instruction over her brood, they seem unaware of my presence. The few sightseers that do make it here, don't notice me at all; they stroll about, bask in the sun, maybe have a picnic, and then head for home.

Except for one man. I see him watching me from time to time; the sunlight catches the warmth of his smile. Perhaps he has news of Francis.

I think about such things when I sit by the river, and wait for my beloved Francis to return.

It's wonderfully peaceful and sultry here, and yet something troubles me … something I've forgotten …

I think it is because I'm not really certain how long I've been waiting for him. Surely he will arrive soon, we are after all, recently married. I hope he's not mad at me for playing that trick on him – the game of hide-and-seek I insisted we play on the day of our wedding. He makes my heart sing with joy when he says how he loves me. I remember how he gazed at me devotedly that night when I was adorned in my beautiful bridal gown – I'm wearing it now just for him. I must be so conspicuous as I wander among the ruins, winter or shine and yet no-one appears to notice me.

This afternoon was different though. As I sat

beside the riverbank with my eyes closed, listening to the sound of birdsong, the buzzing of bees, and the steady trickle of the water's flow, something disturbed me. A dark shadow blotted out the sun, causing me to reopen them abruptly.

"I'm sorry, I didn't mean to startle you, Rebekah."

I jumped. The man – the one with the smile – stood over me.

I rose to my feet, stammering a reply. "Forgive me, it's just that no one usually notices me down here, let alone engages in conversation with me."

Self consciously, I straightened my dress, and brushed away the soil and grass.

"How do you know my name? Has Francis sent you? Do you have news of him?"

He looked so kind and gentle. If it wasn't for that, I'd swear he was a ghost come to haunt me.

"But you sought *me* out, Rebekah. I have the gift to see you … and I want to help you. I'm here to put things right."

"How did you know where to find me?"

"You told me, don't you remember? Through your heart … I can read your thoughts."

"Who are you?"

"You can call me Sam."

"Are you a spirit? A ghost? Are you … *dead*?"

I can hardly believe I asked the question, and I felt scared as to what he would say.

He simply shook his head.

"I'm on the other side of the divide, Rebekah,

yes … but, well … I'm sorry, but you don't understand do you? Well of course not, that's why I'm here I suppose … you see, it's *you* who needs to move on."

"But my husband … I am expecting his return and I'm waiting for him …Where is he? I want him."

He looked sad. "You are unaware of your passing, but it is he who is waiting for *you* on the other side, and he has yearned for you to be with him for a very long time now."

Then he smiled at me again. "Perhaps you would care for a stroll as it's such a lovely summer's afternoon?"

"I would consider that as most agreeable, sir, yes. I confess to be in need of company."

It was so nice to pass the lonely hours in such convivial surroundings, and pleasing to find someone to talk to.

As we traversed the ruins, I became engrossed in the stories he told me. The priory buildings lay under the lawns we walked across, he said, but it had become a manor house since the time of Henry the Eighth and the Reformation. Well, all this came as a surprise to me, because I had never known of a 'Henry the Eighth' or his 'desecration of the monasteries' so described by this gentleman. I assume he was referring to the usurper Henry Tudor's second son. I never concern myself with the politics of state; that would be unseemly for the Lady of a nobleman.

My gentleman companion showed me how the lawns once formed the monks' cloisters, and where the dormitory and refectory once were.

When we arrived at the tower and chimney, I was about to ask if this formed part of the kitchens and bake house, but I noticed his smile had faltered. He urged me to move on, and as I did so, he resumed his affable manner.

We walked to the edge of the grounds and to a wrought iron gate, which overlooked the pasture fields beyond. The river meandered through a thicket of trees, and he told me that if I followed its course, I would discover a dovecote built into the old boundary wall of the priory. He explained that when the abbeys and monasteries were replaced by manor houses, the wealthy owners would often build dovecotes nearby but for their own private use.

He sighed, and then he looked at me."Yes, it was sad when the Lord of the manor died the way he did. Now all is decay, and it is time to move on … we must visit the dovecote. Come, I'll walk with you."

***

I cannot recall what we talked about as we made our way to the dovecote hidden among the trees, except that the man who called himself Sam seemed very kind. He must have left me before I entered the silent void within its walls, because I can no longer sense his presence.

The effulgence of the cloudless sky filtering through the pigeon holes above me cause them to resemble rows of pale blue eyes. They stare at me in the darkness. They want to show me something.

Wait …

My heart skips.

This isn't the dovecote … it is the tower and I am at the top of the narrow winding stairs that lead to our bedchamber. I can hear my feet echo around the stone walls as I climb the steps.

Hah! It makes me laugh at the thought of all those men scurrying around the house and grounds searching for me. What fun! It was my idea of course – games of hide-and-seek! It has been such a wonderful ball, and so balmy a summer's evening – this the night of my wedding. I gaze at them through the window as they dance and sing. And the men in their uniforms, the women in their gowns … they look so fine and splendid … and the lighted candles, the gaiety of the minstrels and the music … a game of hide-and-seek is the perfect way to end this magical day.

But lo, the music has stopped and they have begun their quest. I will climb into the heavy oak chest beside the bed. There, they will never find me …

Ooh … the moment when the clasp clicks shut on the lid I realise how foolish I am.

Help me.

Help me.

I scream and I roar; my eyes stretch wide, roll up, and burst from their sockets. I claw at the oak, and beg for light, and beg for air, and the blood from my broken fingernails soils my gown. The pain in my breast burns me, and my jaw stretches until it cracks and there is no breath left in my lungs to scream anymore.

But suddenly, the blackness all around me brightens, and a soothing luminance bathes and caresses me. My chest stops heaving and my heart ceases pounding … and then … bliss … bliss …

You see, I no longer need to breathe, for my body, wrapped inside my soiled bridal gown lies below me sealed in the box.

I look at the men frantically searching the rooms and grounds of the manor. Night turns to day, and changes to night again, but they continue to search, and they search, and they search …

My husband's peers suggest to him that I have eloped for a secret assignation with a paramour, but my darling Francis refuses to believe them, yet I know he will be forced to succumb …

The days pass by until time no longer has meaning. Francis has stopped searching – he had to. I have despaired at how he has withered and perished. There are no more parties, and the fine buildings of the manor house are crumbling into ruin.

Eventually they find my husband's secret underground chamber, and his body sitting upright at his desk behind the bricked up door. They say he fled there to escape execution, his hiding known only to his servant who failed to return. Francis was a supporter of the Lancastrian cause, and he feared the traitor's axe at the hands of Henry Tudor. But I know different – he could not live without me, his dear Rebekah, and so he died of anguish, hidden from the world.

The tower crumbles and collapses with the passing of the seasons, and far below me I observe the floor and the oak chest crashing to the ground. I watch as the workmen prize open the lock, their countenance awash with curiosity. My brittle, dry bones and wisps of hair spill out onto the ground, still wrapped in my gown, which is stained with my mortal remains.

I look upon the remains - I call them that, for I feel that they are not really a part of me - with disgust. How vile, to think that our souls reside in these bodies, albeit for such a fleeting period. I watch as they bury the bones next to the grave of my husband in the churchyard, near to the manor.

I catch a glimpse of that man called Sam again, walking away into the distance - the man with the smile. He was so kind to have helped me like that.

But as I soar into the brightness above me, with my hair billowing, my dress is white and gleaming pure again. At last I can see my beloved Francis greeting me as I move towards the light.

Bayard's Leap

It is said that at the point of death, the moment when your guardian angel is no longer there to guide and protect you, that your whole life flashes before your eyes and everything is played out in slow motion. The passage of time becomes meaningless. It certainly seemed that way to Henry Bayard as he hung from the scaffolding one hundred feet above ground. He had jumped from the tower just as she had instructed him to do. A leap of faith Meg had called it; well, he didnt have much faith now, and thus, he regretted the last decision he would ever make. Indeed, he regretted all his actions over the past few hours; they seemed so pointless and absurd – just as clinging to a rusty iron girder with one set of fingers, and with his arm being wrenched out of its socket, was also absurd. In a moment he would succumb to the excruciating pain and he would lose his tenuous grip; the creaking structure would collapse, and send both him and the girders tumbling into the darkness.

In that moment his life did indeed flash before him, or at least, the day's events that had led to his downfall ....

It had been around mid-morning when he'd arrived at the diner with Meg. Their presence had disturbed the leafy quiet with a crunching of tyres on gravel from her convertible sports car, all red and shiny with black trimmings, and gleaming in the summer sun. The car reminded him of a wild and untamed panther, dangerous and feral, and mimicking its owner. Somehow he had managed to persuade the girl of his dreams to spend the day with him - but he had no game plan as to where he would take her.

"We should take to the highway and see where it leads," she announced in her customary forthright manner. Her forcefulness appealed to him and besides, he was way below her league, so he would do anything to please her in the hope of making a good impression.

Bayard's Leap Café - tucked away on the corner where the Ancaster road ended, and joined the busy modern thoroughfare heading to Norfolk and the coast. It nestled amid a row of dilapidated work buildings set beside a disused trackway and crossroads, which were sheltered from the noise and pollution of the noisy drone of passing traffic by a curtain of trees and wild hedgerows.

He'd known of its existence from the books he'd read. It stood on the site of a famous local legend concerning a witch, but hadn't got around to stopping there. The fact that both Henry and the café bore the same name, 'Bayard', was not lost on him. Its location beside the old Roman route known as Ermine Street, 'The Great North Road', with its inevitable legends and tales of ghostly airfields, Roman legionaries, and will o' the wisps - not to mention the tale of Bayard's leap itself - fired his imagination, and was the perfect setting in which to insinuate his fantasy goddess.

For the Romans, the highway had formed a lifeline for troops and supplies from London to Lincoln and York. Now it was a haunt for bikers and lorry drivers, so he had never mustered up the courage to stop and explore.

She told him she was hungry, and that they should stop off somewhere. Bayard's Leap Café beckoned, and it was too good an opportunity to miss.

She was the first to step out of the car - of course - followed by a meek and fainthearted Henry. She turned her back to him, stole him a glimpse from over her shoulder, and cast a knowing smile, but her eyes were masked by the sunglasses. He was afraid she'd hear him sigh - she mesmerised him; those skintight hipsters and silver calf-length boots outlined the shape of her long legs and perfectly formed buttocks beautifully. The way she swaggered towards the café entrance left him spellbound - and she knew it.

He followed her. He always followed her.

It was as he expected it to be - an old-fashioned diner furnished with ornate tables and chairs, checkered tablecloths, sets of cruet, sauce bottles, and quaint handwritten menu cards. It was a small, quiet room, enclosed by pretty, curtained latticed windows, and was deserted, save for an elderly couple sitting in the corner sipping tea, who looked upon the new arrivals with suspicion, lest their peace and quiet be disturbed.

The newcomers eyed the morsels under the

glass counter, but no-one emerged from the kitchen beyond to greet them. Henry screwed his nose up at the cakes and flans inside the glass with angst, searching for flies and creepy crawlies.

"Don't be such a woos, Henry!" Meg admonished him from behind the sunglasses, *"I'm hungry."* Her head turned to the menu written in chalk on a board. "Hmm … Egg and chips, ham and chips, ham, egg and chips, sausage and chips, sausage, egg and chips, fish and chips, or just chips; peas, bread and butter extra …." She pursed her bright red lips "A problem then if you don't like chips."

She threw him a withering glance. He could sense her disappointment, her *disgust*, and it was aimed at him; he felt so inadequate. She shouted for service, and a young waitress with an apron, a sour face, and hair as greasy as the menu, appeared from behind a curtain. Any fear Henry had that the girl may take exception to this inconvenient intrusion vanished, because Meg - forceful Meg - was in control.

"I'll have ham, egg and chips please; ***I'm hungry***," she said.

"Er, I'll have the same." Henry could not decide. "Oh, and er … two teas?"

"No, *you* have tea, sweetheart, you're driving this afternoon; I'll have a cold beer."

The girl with the sour face scribbled the order on her pad, and disappeared behind the curtain again.

Meg studied the room, weighing up as to

whether the establishment met with her approval; the dark glasses accentuating her superior air, hiding her true intent. She sniffed.

"We'll eat outside on the terrace … take in the sun and fresh air." She made for the door, hips swaggering. "Don't forget the knives and forks, lover!"

The pensioners shook their heads with disapproval.

They sat for the most part in silence as they ate their meal. Meg seemed content to soak up the warming, balmy breeze as it rustled through the canopy of leafy trees that protected them from the road beyond. Not a living soul disturbed them.

The trouble was, he could never tell what she was looking at behind those shades, all black and glistening in the sun: the garden shop next door, the disused petrol pump standing crooked, and strewn with old tyres from a burnt out van nearby … or the row of single storey motel rooms lying just beyond. He gulped at such a delicious thought.

Perhaps she was merely enjoying the solitude.

"No, she's bored … ***bored****. Any minute now she'll insist on going home – she'll issue the command. I've blown my big chance with her."*

The roar of approaching motorbikes shattered the idyll. He jumped, waiting in dreaded apprehension, as two … three … four of them appeared from the other side of the trees, rearing onto the gravel path; a cacophony of chugging and backfiring, and spewing pungent fumes. They circled malevolently. Meg's face lit up, a smile curled on her lips and he despaired when he saw how the noisy intrusion had excited her. The leather clad bikers removed their helmets, dismounted and headed for the café entrance, turning their heads towards her, grinning, strutting and posturing.

She beamed at them, and when her lips parted, he saw her teeth - the sun caught their gleam - white, perfectly formed … and sharp. Then, for some reason, he could not stop looking at her teeth.

They passed by and entered the diner, much to Henry's relief, but he was fearful they would reappear at any moment.

She licked her blood-red lips as the last slice of bacon from her plate slithered down her throat. "Mmm … reminds me of the Wild West … a diner, a motel, a run-down garage, bikers …." She paused, slowly settling her blank, expressionless visage on him. She was studying him in that cool, familiar aloof manner. But it thrilled him.

"You can't take your eyes off me, can you?" she teased.

It was true; he was totally transfixed. The brightness of the day transformed her thick, blonde shoulder-length hair, translucent in the breeze … and heightened her ample breasts, scarcely concealed under the stretched fabric of her tee-shirt; her striking appearance was spellbinding. Then, there were the fingernails, so long and tapering, and as blood-red as her lips. He'd first caught sight of them in the car when they had grasped the gear lever. But it was the hidden eyes; how he wished he could unravel the mystery of her eyes ….

He sighed once more. He wanted her so much, and in the most base of ways. He would do anything if he thought he was in with a chance.

Her smile dropped suddenly, putting him on edge again.

"So where are you taking me then?" she demanded.

"Well, I hadn't really thought … there's always the coast … or perhaps we could take in the history … we could go for a walk along Ermine Street; it leaves the road, and forms a trackway north of the crossroads—"

She laughed aloud, "Oh, Henry! 'go for a walk, take in the history' - you're such a geek; a gal like me wants excitement!"

She tossed her head back, and thrust out her chest.

"Yes … a geek; that's what you are. I bet you're a fan of Star Trek, aren't you … all of it, yes. You have the box set?"

He felt himself redden. Her chuckles subsided, leaving the mocking grin and bared white teeth.

"Oh, Henry, you *are* a poppet!"

"Yet, you're here with me, aren't you. You didn't have to come out with me."

She drew a deep breath, and lifted up her chin. He swore her nostrils twitched and he thought of an animal hunting its prey.

"You're scheming to enter my bed, aren't you?

Forming a plan, finding a route … seeking permission, the ultimate accolade."

She cocked a pencil-thin eyebrow, and leant forward, placing her hand on his; her face so close that he could feel her breath. He went crimson.

She lowered her voice. "There's a motel 'cross there. You want to book a room?"

A lump formed in his throat and he swallowed. She was teasing him … wasn't she?

Then she backed away, and sniggered. "But, Henry Bayard, you'll have to do better than this."

She slumped back on her chair and raised her beer bottle when the hells angels re-emerged.

"Let me think what I want you to do for me … and, well, if you impress, you never know, you might just get your leg over."

So he was still in with a chance! Henry's heart thumped as the motorbikes' ignitions and revving engines cracked like thunder.

She watched them as they disappeared beyond the trees and headed off down the unseen highway to Ancaster, the commotion fading in the breeze.

"But in the meantime, while I'm thinking … tell me a ghost story."

"What?"

"Well, that's the other reason you've come here to Bayard's Leap isn't it? Besides wanting to lay me … the ghosts, the folklore? I don't need to go for walks, just tell me."

"Right, well um … you know about the legend of Bayard's Leap and the witch … at least I think you do, so I won't bother you with that one .... There's the ghost of the airman said to haunt this area. You see, the Ancaster road forms part of the old Roman supply route we call Ermine Street, the name Ermine deriving from the word 'Ermingas', the title given to the people inhabiting the Cambridge area. It became one of the few Saxon roads—"

"Boring, ***boorring!***"

"Sorry...well, er, anyway this pilot was stationed at the airfield, here behind these trees on the other side of The Great *East* Road. The land opens up after you leave this wooded valley and the terrain is littered with airstrips, hangars and buildings from the 1940s."

Meg appeared to be staring impassively into the laden boughs waving in the sighing breeze - the sun glinting on her face and glasses, masking her expression - and he was unsure whether she was listening. He assumed that she was.

"He was known as 'Jack the Lad', and during the last war, he and his comrades would often drive down into Ancaster of an evening in search of beer and women - they treated each day as their last. Jack was the worst of the womanisers, and inevitably one of the local lasses became quite enamoured of him. She was supposed to have lived in a cottage on the heath not far from here, with two other women. Though not exactly outcasts, no-one really knew much about them, but by all accounts, she was a bit simple. But she was fair, pretty, and had a heart of gold, and so was easy pickings for our Jack. Rumours got around that she was expecting his child but he had no intention of standing by her, and for reasons that have never been adequately resolved, he took her out into the woods one night to explain that he was leaving her. She was later found dead - stabbed through the heart - but, and this is the odd thing, her body and clothes were charred and burnt.

"He wrote in his diary that very night that it was she who had intended to kill him, following a fit of grief when he told her of his intentions. Tempers rose but they were interrupted by what he described as 'a dark, and shapeless phantom', and the sound of a whinnying and baying horse in distress. Inexplicably, she had turned the knife on herself, before combusting in front of his very eyes. You hear about that sort of thing, don't you? The flames were said to have shone with a blue-white, cold hue; a ghostly torch flame glowing in the forest.

"Anyway, overcome by terror and confusion, he fled, and made his way back to the airfield. He scribbled the account in his diary, and then took off in his plane. It was a Hurricane fighter you know....

"Er, sorry ... of course, he'd forgotten that the plane hadn't been serviced and fuelled, and according to the reports, it ditched somewhere over the North Sea, and he was killed, or drowned ... which was just as well because he would surely have hanged had they caught him.

"So, the ghost of 'Jack the Lad' is doomed to haunt these woods, as is the black horse, and the 'white woman of flames' as she is called - often described as a will o'the wisp. Venture into them at your peril, because if you ever hear the sound of muffled arguing and crying, then all three phantoms will be upon you. The black shape and whinnying is one thing, but if you are unfortunate and catch plain sight of the horse, your death is sure to follow. Maybe that's what happened to the pilot."

Meg seemed unmoved and continued to gaze at the swaying trees, deep in thought. Perhaps she had lost interest.

She suddenly turned and studied him, her visage a pale gleaming disc in the bright, and the teeth emerged again, parting the glossy, red lips, and betraying a half-smile.

"I know … three dares … I'll give you three dares, and if you succeed …" she pointed to the motel with her finger and the long, blood-red nail.

Henry blushed hot. He realised how stupid he must have looked with his mouth agape, and his power of speech rendered useless.

"The first dare is quite simple: we leave here without paying for our meal."

"What? You mean, not paying … no, it's not right, not right."

She rose abruptly from her chair and strode towards the car.

"Oh, well if you can't pass the most basic of dares, then I'm going home right now. Do you want a lift or not?"

"No, no wait, OK, OK we'll do it … you mean … just sneak off without a word?"

"There's no sneaking off about it, flower, they are hardly in a position to do anything about it are they? We drive off, and that's that. And don't forget, you're doing the driving."

She tossed the keys at him, which he almost dropped as the unexpected missile struck him in the midriff.

And with a screech of the tyres, and a crunching of gravel, they fled from the diner and hit the tarmac.

"Which way?" he pleaded as he halted at the lay-by entrance, feeling inadequate again. How he wished he could see behind the sunglasses; behind the cold, withering stare.

"Drive towards Ancaster … and this is your second dare … I want you to really open up the throttle … thrill me, excite me, let's feel some speed!"

He crunched the gears, shot into reverse and stalled the engine. The car lurched forward onto the highway and he wrestled with the steering wheel.

He cringed at his inadequacy. "N-not used to the controls … so powerful; runs away with you. I'll soon get the hang … s-see if I don't …."

He knew this long stretch of straight road, with its humps and dips, was known locally as North Dyke. Meg glowered at him with a look of cruelty, disgust and loathing, but he failed to notice because he was so intent on taming the vehicle. Of that he was spared; it would have destroyed him for certain.

There were few fellow travellers on the carriageway. He was hoping one of the many slow moving military convoys that still used it would turn up, and then all bets would be off. No such luck. The force of the revs vibrated on his gripping hands, and into his bones as the car gained speed. He glanced at the speedometer.

Fifty … sixty…

The engine roared, and to his surprise he got a kick. "OK … this is OK."

He dared a sideways glimpse at his passenger, but her mouth was downturned and she glared ahead with an icy, cold-hearted stare as chilling as the wind whistling in his ears.

"You've got to go faster than this, *much* faster," she commanded.

"I'm … I'm not used to the power of a motor like this." He squeezed the pedal, the engine roared louder making him gasp. The needle on the dial climbed steadily.

Sixty … seventy …

His knuckles whitened as he gripped the wheel harder. Beads of sweat itched on his forehead, in spite of the fierce cold air current lashing his face and rippling through his shirt. His throat went dry. Cars from the opposite direction rushed by in a blur.

"Faster … faster!"

"I can't … I can't … the road, it dips … the double white lines … what if there's something hidden in the dips?"

"*Faster … faster…*" and he could hear her laughter.

He threw her another sideways glance in desperation and caught the shock of thick, blonde hair dancing in the wind, and the glasses, and the teeth … laughing.

… Laughing at the way he lurched in his seat, jolting and bumping, dipping and rising in the hollows.

Seventy … eighty …

The engine thundered. Henry held on for dear life. The red warning signs, 'Hidden dips', 'Concealed crossroads' whizzed by, and then a third: 'Low bridge, two miles'. They were fast approaching the town.

"We …we'll never stop in time!"

Over the next rise, the motorbikes loomed ahead - distant but they were closing in on them.

"***Faster … faster!***" Her nose was raised and her teeth gleamed, and her bark was more akin to a lupine howl.

They were gaining on them, slowly ….

The car buffeted, the speed dial rose. He saw one rider turn his shiny metal head around; they'd been spotted.

"Do it, Henry … *do it now!*"

He either had to 'take' them, or slow down and lose face … and suffer the wrath of the she-monster beside him.

Eighty … ninety …

His foot met the floorboard. The noise of the motor screeched ever louder.

He 'took' the first bike, and it buzzed by in a split-second like an angry bluebottle. Then came the second … then the third.

Another sign: 'Low Bridge one mile'.

He sweated and prayed there was nothing coming the other way. The fourth bluebottle stubbornly refused to get closer, but he was committed. He was on the wrong side of the road, and there was no way back.

Ninety … ninety-five …

At last the biker acquiesced, and slowly, agonizingly slowly … he passed it.

There was only one left now – the leader – still no more than a black shape, shimmering in the bright afternoon sun. It disappeared under the railway bridge. Henry sensed the blur of buildings, houses and people shoot by, just at the point of his losing his reason.

Then she did it.

She slammed her palm onto his thigh, and it stung.

"Stop … Stop now!"

He lost control. He slammed his foot on the brake, the tyres screeched, and the car shuddered and weaved all over the highway as he desperately grappled with the steering wheel. His heart pounded and his mind reeled with a rush of blurred images flashing before him.

Somehow, he did not know how, the vehicle ceased its spin and shuddered to a halt. He felt his head hit the rest, hard. The sky and the buildings stopped whirling, but his heart continued to race. The car had spun full circle, and, with her uproarious and merciless laughter ringing in his ears, not even the rush of a train hurtling over the steel bridge above them could drown it.

His fingers still clutched the wheel … with hers – the blood-red talons – resting on his. So he *had* lost control, and it was she who had saved them.

She leant into him and loomed. Her cackles ceased abruptly, and with a feeling of submission and despair, he saw the cool smile accentuated by those damnable shades return. Her talons dropped, and struck him in the groin. He winced.

"Mmm, that made me feel so ***good*** …"

She sucked the air in through her teeth, and squeezed her hand round his crotch. His eyes popped and he flinched, uttering a cry; complete subjugation and at her mercy.

The rumble of the approaching motorbikes distracted them and broke the spell. The riders of the highway did not appreciate this unexpected challenge. North Dyke was after all, their territory.

She chuckled. "Don't you think that it might be a good idea if we were to leave, Henry? How convenient for the car to turn around full circle; we'll head back in the direction we came. It's all right, chicken, you can drive at a nice steady pace now if you feel safer; you've passed the second dare."

Forty … fifty … forty …

This time it was the turn of the bikers to overtake *them*, but only after a great deal of posturing, revving of engines and swaggering, and a considerable degree of confrontational finger wagging. He thought it best not to make eye contact, and fixed his gaze on the road ahead. Meg beamed at them, waving her arm. They guffawed and wolf-whistled, until finally they drove on, gradually disappearing in the distance.

Henry brooded. He had travelled the North Dyke before, though never like this. His humiliation morphed to resentment; he reminded himself he wasn't a complete wimp. "You realise that we could have been killed back there if I had lost control? What if something had been coming the other way … and the houses? What if there had been a tractor hidden in one of the dips? What if—"

Another chuckle cut him short.

"Oh, babe, you never *were* in control; I was all along, just as I am now."

"What do you mean by that?"

She kept him hanging; her expression still concealed by the shades. She was pondering … deciding what she would do with him. Then, she licked her lips, and with a curious, guttural exhalation of her breath, answered him in a sultry tone - the type that excited Henry.

"Drive us back to Bayard's Leap, and I'll book us a room. Don't worry about the café owner, or any of the bikers, I'll tell them that it was all my doing. Then, if you pass the third and final dare, you can have me … my body, my flesh, all to yourself, all night long or until you are sated … I know that is what you want."

His indignation melted in an instant, thus proving that she was indeed in control.

***

Such were the events that led Henry Bayard to his doom.

... To the deserted and ramshackle aerodrome at dusk, and the dark tower outlined on the horizon.

No thought, no ambition, other than that of the supreme accolade of seeing Meg naked and bedding her would have driven him into undertaking so absurd a folly. She had given him precise instructions for his final dare, and he knew exactly what he had to do. He was just one step away, just one step ....

It hadn't occurred to him that he had no means of proving he had accomplished the task; he was simply relying on faith - blind faith - that she would know.

The abandoned airfield lay to the north of the highway and Bayard's Leap, both of which hid in the wooded valley. Out here, the Lincolnshire fens painted a different world, that of a vast, imposing expanse, dominated by the tall, brooding fortress, silhouetted against a rose-red sunset sky.

To its side, leaned a patchwork of dilapidated, rusty scaffolding and platforms. The edifice, dating from the fifteenth century - Henry knew the local history well - had doubled as a conning and signalling tower during the Second World War, and the scaffolding no doubt acted as some kind of appendage to the building. He was surprised that it remained intact after decades of abandonment and neglect; it must surely be unsafe. Yet this was what stood between him and his goal. All he had to do was climb the steps of the tower from within, and make the leap across the gap between it and the iron structure. He could then climb down the girders, and so complete the third dare. Simple!

He recalled his day at the library and what he gleaned from its dusty tomes. The tower was far older than the aerodrome. Typical of the fifteenth century, it was built to impress upon the locals, both the symbolic and absolute hegemony that the baron held over them. It certainly impressed Henry. He drew close and craned his neck skywards, looking in awe at the six storeys and walls towering a hundred feet above him and to the crenelated turrets at each corner. Of course, being of brick, it could not have withstood any real conflict of sieges and warfare from the late medieval, but merely the sight of its dominating presence would have been enough to impose the Baron's will.

But the light was fading and he felt uneasy. The silence closed in on him – the hum of the traffic seemed so far away – and the occasional lulling of bleating sheep on the surrounding grassland juxtaposed the rumble of thunder on the distant horizon. He listened and he watched the approaching storm clouds spew their dark tendrils of vapour and taint the sky's canvas of azure and rose-pink. He likened the display to a blackened shape of a squid waiting to pounce from its lair. A deep sense of foreboding swept over him; something malevolent was threatening to weaken his resolve. That is, until he heard her voice emanating from inside the fortress … or his mind … it was difficult to tell.

She was waiting for him and willing him on. She told him that it would be stupid to back out now. He had come so far, and the prize was too great.

He stepped into the abyss.

The darkness hit him, as did the familiar smell of cow dung. This once prestigious fortified home to the earls and barons of Lincoln had been reduced in status to that of a cattle shed. He switched on the torch of his phone – it's all he had, he was so unprepared for the events that had overtook him – and its brilliant, thin beam punched a tiny hole through the blackness.

He peered into the inky void; the silence was suffocating. A grand and ornate stone fireplace, decorated with family shields and heraldry shimmered in the ray. The magnificent entrance hall from that long forgotten time, lay broken and dilapidated. He waved the beam around the chamber, searching. Its limit barely reached the walls, and caused his shadow to dance and flit; a macabre manifestation of his creeping apprehension.

There at the opposite corner … the base of the stone spiral staircase. He extinguished the torch, mindful that its power may soon be exhausted. He called out for Meg; no answer.

He began the ascent, steeling himself for the task and determining not to hurry, otherwise fear and panic would get the better of him. As he passed each floor he averted his eyes from the corridors that led to the labyrinths of passageways and halls, trying not to think upon what dwelled within. Any ghosts and phantoms, should they exist, would surely be awoken by the echoes of his footsteps and his laboured breaths resounding in the hollow emptiness of the pitch.

He must keep moving and not lose count of the floors he passed otherwise he would become disorientated. He had to concentrate, stay alert, and keep a grip on things, and above all, on no account, should he look into the passageways. "Get in and get out, Henry Bayard," he told himself.

And he was doing fine until he paused at the fifth floor, catching his breath. He switched the torch back on – he must have light, he must *see* …

The ray danced and shot down the corridor before he could steady it. A black and shapeless form hovered close by, suspended in the beam. He froze, rooted to the spot.

What the hell is that?

An entity – my god, yes …

He gazed at the phantom transfixed; he was a rabbit caught in the headlights. The entity wobbled and shivered, floating and seeming to drift one way, then the other. He thought he could hear a whinny and a snort; it had sentience.

Please God, don't let it see me; make it go away.

A scream pierced the air and he dropped the torch – his precious source of light. The wail's echo rang hollow, refusing to die; a banshee, screaming among the walls. He cowered, covering his ears. He was aware of muffled and agitated voices emanating from the corridor and hallway beyond … and also the clatter of hooves.

Eventually the cries began to fade and he dared release his grip on his ears. Where was the torch? Where was the light?

He scrambled round him, still crouching, with arms stretched, and groping in the dark. He lost his footing and kicked the fallen object from underneath him. It bounced and clattered down the steps into the nothingness below him … until those echoes also faded, and he was left with that encroaching, dreadful silence once more.

There *was* a source of light, but not from the torch … an incandescent globe gliding into the shadowy depths of the corridor. He gawped, in spite of his rising terror. Inside the glowing, shimmering orb he saw a woman, her robes draped in flames so bright, and yet they did not consume her. But as she floated silently on into the distant unseen hall, she faded, and his world returned to the interminable dark.

He knew that if he descended the spiral steps, his fear would win, he would rush, and he would fall. He had no choice now; the only way out was up.

He made it. Forget the ghost; he would make the leap and accomplish the dare.

He took stock of his surroundings. The flat roof resembled a courtyard, curtained by a raised platform running alongside the crenelated perimeter. Turrets at each corner reached high into the pitch sky. The broken glass, oil drums and rusted metal and wire that littered the floor, and scarcely visible in the twilight, were tell-tale signs of the air force's recent use of the building. The crooked framework of the signalling tower leaned just a hair's breadth beyond the wall … daring him to make the leap.

Shadows cast blackened pools among the boundary edges and turrets. He climbed the nearest steps and mounted the platform, and peeped over the edge. He watched the headlights of the silent cars snaking along the distant highway; a creeping, luminous worm. How he wished he could return to their world. He rued the times when he shunned the parties, the crowds, the people. He felt so lonely and isolated.

These were the last rational thoughts of Henry Bayard.

A movement from the turret at the far end … someone, *something*, had emerged into the open courtyard … but then it disappeared into the shadows.

The moon unveiled herself, sudden and unexpected, splitting through the invisible clouds, and bathing the yard in a pale sheen. His eyes searched frantically across the roof's flattened surface, scanning for any signs of movement. There – an upright figure with a mane of hair – a female. She crept, she stooped, she crouched – a huntress seeking her prey.

He lost her again, hidden in a recess by the wall. He edged away, his bowels loosening, sweat prickling; he had to hide. It re-emerged, climbing on to the platform; so close now. It hovered with its head and mane raised in the air, sniffing for his scent and waiting for him to move and betray his presence.

Then, one of the shadows - darker than the rest - *moved* ... a creeping, swelling sentience. It burst into a fiery ball of spurting stars, silent and awful. Next came a wail, unearthly and piercing; baying, snorting, whinnying. A shape began to form from within - a brute with four legs and a muzzle - a horse wheezing puffs of luminous vapour, and a figure mounted on its hide. And it was black, so black, except for the chain mail borne by the warrior; it shimmered and glistened in the moonlight, mirroring the beast's eyes.

The wolf creature cocked its head, sensing the intrusion. The expression was familiar. She cowered; the hunter had become the prey, and as the spectre brandished its sword, she fled along the wall ... and towards Henry.

He pressed himself against the turret, terror-stricken; she'd disappeared again. The full Moon had risen over the parapet, and hovered - a huge, reddened and distorted ball, low on the horizon. The hollow echoes of the knight and his steed's clopping hooves rang in the ether. His heart thumped and he felt sick. Where was the creature? He was certain it was coming straight at him.

She'll be on me at any mo—

A rearing head silhouetted against the disc of the moon, and looming, its hot breath wetting his skin. He lurched back and banged his skull on the wall. He struggled to focus but he could still see the voluminous mane of thick hair, as the beast stood erect ...

It was human! It was Meg. She *had* followed him there and was playing games with him. He grinned stupidly.

The shades were gone, but when - finally - he saw her eyes he fell to his knees and cringed before her in terror. The bright yellow beads were lupine with narrow vertical slats for pupils - those of a wolf. The blood-red fingernails had morphed to claws, and her teeth were fangs - sharp, white and drooling saliva.

And she was naked at last … but grey and pocked with wispy patches of fur.

He sidled along the wall, quailing, but she suddenly roared and lashed out with her talons. He tripped and toppled over the edge.

Not enough time to convert the fall into a leap - that fabled leap - but his fingers caught the jutting pole of the scaffolding that protruded a few feet from the wall.

He clung, hanging on for precious life, with his fingers and arm socket at breaking point. All those notions of Meg and her warm bed seemed so remote now; how superfluous and absurd his actions had been.

He heard the ensuing conflagration on the rooftop. The knight and his steed had cornered the wolf creature. With a snarl, a growl and a scream, she leapt from the tower, her body impaled by the sword, its silhouette captured in the backdrop of the moon. She pounced onto Henry's leg, howling and hissing. As her claws dug into his thigh, she emitted a final, blood-curdling growl from her downturned mouth, as her body twitched and jerked in the moonlight.

That was enough. The searing pain caused his grip to falter, and with a crash and a clatter that he was unable to comprehend, the scaffolding gave way, sending him, Meg and the iron bars plunging into oblivion.

Yes … the proof was there for Henry at the point of death; time no longer had meaning; it no longer followed the normal rules.

As he dropped, the whole legend of Bayard's Leap that he'd learned of as a boy played out to him like a storybook …

Once, in a past and distant age, when the land and the people were plagued by civil war waged by the great royal households, there lived a black witch. She came from a cottage somewhere on Sparrow Gorse. She is said to have raised two wolf cubs, and she treated them as if they were her own.

She would torment travellers who used the old north road that crossed the heath by robbing and harassing them, and would assume the form of a crone, a voluptuous woman, or a banshee. She also tainted the peasants' corn stock, and on one occasion, caused the cattle to die of a sudden, and mysterious illness.

So much did she harry the locals that, so the legend goes, the three white witches who also dwelt on the heath, decided that they should cleanse her of all her wickedness and wrongdoings.

The most wise and beautiful of the white witches was the first to enter the black witch's cottage, but she was cast outside again by the curses and utterances of the evil crone. They were so obscene that it caused an eruption of boils and sores to blight the noble white witch's entire face and body. They were so severe that no-one would go near her, and so she died of loneliness.

The second of the white witches also approached the cottage, but she was struck by a bolt of lightning and thrown a hundred feet into the sky. She fell back to the earth into the black witch's well, said to be so deep it was bottomless. Her body was never found.

That left the third white witch. She was the youngest and fairest but proved no threat at all to the evil grimalkin. She drew her into her cottage, and manacled and enslaved her.

When he heard about these events, the local baron, the wealthy landowner and treasurer to the boy-King Henry VI, took upon himself to liberate the people by promising to kill the black witch. He would also rescue the fair maiden and make her his bride. They would live at the grand castle fortress he had recently built on the open land. He was a veteran from the times of the French wars, and feared no-one, or nothing in combat.

The citizens were hopeful.

In order to perform the deed, he would require a horse, the bravest and most battle hardened that he possessed. But which one? One evening, after having fed his animals, he led them to the pond to drink, whereupon he had an idea. He would toss a pebble into the water, and the first steed to raise its head would be the one he chose. However, when he threw the stone, the first to lift its muzzle was 'Blind Bayard', but he was reluctant to employ the horse, because although he was the bravest and most loyal, he was aged and quite blind.

So, the baron repeated the ritual the next evening, but again 'Blind Bayard' was the first to lift his head. The third evening produced the same result, so he knew he should take the old horse with him.

The following morning, he saddled 'Blind Bayard', donned his chain mail, sharpened his sword, and rode out to the witch's cottage.

"Witch, come out and show yourself, and prepare to die," he yelled.

But the witch shouted back at him:

"I'll buckle me' shoes an' suckle me' cubs, then I'll come out an' put a curse on yer."

As soon as she emerged, the knight struck at her with his sword and split her breast. She flew into a rage, and with her thick hair flying in the wind, her teeth gnashing, and with her yellow, beady eyes that would stun any normal man, she flew at 'Blind Bayard's' flank and dug her blood-red nails – fingers and toes – into his flesh. The pain caused Bayard to leap into the air, and as he did so, he left a single horseshoe behind. On his second leap he dropped another shoe one hundred yards distant, and, at the third leap, he did the same.

Then, the knight took a mighty thrust at the black witch who was still clinging on and digging into Bayard's side. He missed and caught the horse, and the blow was so powerful that it killed Bayard instantly. The witch had fallen, but as the noble beast collapsed, it fell on to her and squashed her to death. With a final moan, she drew her last breath.

On walking back to the cottage, the knight hunted down the half-human, half-wolf infants and put them to the sword, and, so as to purge the land of all evil, he set fire to the dwelling. But in his single mindedness, he had forgotten about the third, and the fairest of the white witches. As the fire raged, she fled in a pall of flames, and in her dying anguish she vowed that she would haunt the baron's domain, and return many times to break the hearts and souls of men.

The leap of Bayard was supposed to have stretched over three hundred yards, but nothing is left of the hoof marks or of the horseshoes. Yet it is said, that the horse, the black witch, and her two cubs are buried under a stone to the south of the old crossroads where a travellers' rest now lies.

This, give or take, was as Henry remembered, the legend of Bayard's Leap.

Then he remembered the name of the black witch.

It was Meg.

He could see the tendrils of the storm clouds sailing swiftly across the sky; their darkening reds and blues would soon be blotted out by night and rain.

But he was unsure whether he was falling or floating above them, high in the firmament, because the full moon still shone brightly. He *was* aware of Meg's body with its soft, warm delights underneath embracing him.

The moon, mimicking a huge eye or a light from a tunnel, drew him as he drifted towards its radiance.

Tower of Silence

A state of utter contentment has imbued me on this still, summer's evening, and its all down to Zoë my still-life model as I like to call her. There's something about her; her presence excites me. She's like the humid air hanging in the reddening light when the sun sets. Her sultry essence leaves me hot and breathless.

But sated, nevertheless.

She was very accommodating this afternoon when she sat and posed for me on the grassy mound beneath the leafy boughs, wearing her familiar smile, and not uttering a word. The brushstrokes upon the canvas had come thick and fast, and all the while she gazed at me with her lazy, affable eyes.

I can see the hill where we pass the time from the window of the cabin right now. I knew this was the right place to moor the barge: a mile or so down a lonely tributary off the river Kennet, under the shade of a willow. There's a perfect view of the gentle rolling hills of the countryside, with the old barrow crowned by ash trees and blackened by the pink sky. That's where she sits for me.

Such a satisfying day. The skylarks had sung their euphony high above us as they flitted and hovered in the open, in spite of the heat. It was so humid, even over there in the shelter of the trees; it made the sweat on my brow feel sticky. But Zoë never complained and I realised how lucky I was as I worked away at the easel. She lounged against a trunk clad in her skin-tight jeans, splaying her long legs, and with her head tilted to one side. She stared and smiled at me with her familiar, passive air.

She indulged my every whim as I talked about this and that, and, after a while, I'd felt emboldened enough to be a little more daring:

"I wondered," my voice broke slightly as a lump formed in my throat, "if we were to unbutton your jacket a little more … and allow the sunlight filtering through the leaves overhead to give your flesh tones more life … it unveils such a lovely golden colour."

She said nothing, of course. I would have to show her what I meant, but just as I walked towards her, a breeze unsettled the heavy leafed boughs above, and the resulting shimmering sunrays caused myriad medallions of gold to cascade over her. Her face seemed curiously animated, her eyebrows puckered, and her lips appeared to move as though to say, "Yes … if it pleases you."

And I remember the caw of a carrion crow suffocating the song of the skylarks as she did so.

Not wishing to upset her faultless poise, I unbuttoned her denim jacket to the waist, revealing the ripeness of her breast and suppleness of her flesh. "Perfect," I thought and continued to paint.

We must have sat there for hours; her patience was admirable. Eventually, my skin began to itch with the heat, and flying insects buzzed and wined all around us. They were settling on our skin, and I could feel them feasting on the salt from my sweat. The evening air lay heavy. Fingers of shadows were settling among the trees where light once breathed, and the colours around us were fading.

I looked around me anxiously. Anyone out for a stroll before supper might get the wrong idea if they spotted us up here. OK so this was art but they wouldn't understand, would they?

I looked back at the exquisite form before me, and to the shape of her legs sprawled in front of her amid the grass - a form, I know, that will soon be corrupted; it compels me to finish my work.

"Till tomorrow then?"

She smiled back from within the shadows, the golden light having faded, and turned her flesh a pallid grey. The skylarks no longer sang, and even the crows were listless; they seemed to accept the coming darkness.

That was a couple of hours ago. As I stare out of the cabin window, the blackened outline of the trees against the blood-red sunset is all that I can see of the hill - the place of our tryst.

Soon the vision will come, just as it did last night, and the night before…

Soon …

There …

The trees have disappeared, and so have the fields. The river, once sluggish and lazy, now sprawls mighty and wide. The hill, denuded of greenery, dominates the skyline and overlooks a vast plain. A huge tower of felled logs and branches, bound together with reeds and twine, juts into the sky akin to a giant clothes maiden. Its struts are black amid the backdrop of the blazing firmament.

Crows circle overhead. A feeling of desolation and depression has washed over me, and my mood is sullen.

There are rows of human bodies silhouetted against the sky, suspended from the crossbeams of the racked tower. The lifeless forms hang inert – abandoned and forgotten like broken mannequins, or puppets from a macabre children's seaside show.

Then, as I curl up in my bunk beneath the cabin window and close my eyes, I travel there. I can see some of their faces, where faces still exist, and there are traces of dried and shrivelled tissue – a taut membrane stretched across cheekbones and gaping mouths. The eyes, wide and hollow, have long since been pecked out. Others are just bone and carcass; the decaying flesh and entrails washed away by wind and rain.

There are similar towers in the valley beyond, but it's this one I'm drawn to. I watch the still, and oh, so silent corpses bound to the rack as they fall to earth … when the shrunken, denuded bones slip from the bindings and tumble to the ground; one by one, limb by limb. And yet the shapes and forms remain suspended on the rack as an after-image. They animate and engage in ritual.

The dance of the dead.

They remind me of scarecrows – the same broad crocodile smile – except unlike scarecrows, they are *attracting* the crows. Later, in the dark of night, it will be the turn of the scavengers - the rodents that scurry up the posts and gnaw hungrily at the carrion.

Last night, in my vision, a raft approached and moored alongside the tower. I was too far distant to hear anything, but they hauled two fresh corpses onto the platform. The Zoroastrian priests watched the ceremony with cold and bleak expressions. I know that's what they call themselves because I'd read about them before I went to sleep. They dispose of their dead by placing them on such edifices, so that birds of prey and scavengers can strip the flesh from the bones. Only then will their souls be purified and free to travel and dwell underground to the realm of the afterlife. Eventually, they'll burn the bones and inter them in the sacred barrows - such as the one on the hill now, but they'll resurrect them again - many times - in future rituals to be performed by their descendants. They're seeking wisdom and guidance from their ancestors residing in the domain of the hereafter - that's what I read. Rites of necromancy, performed by the believers. They're called Parsees. Only when no-one believes anymore, can the dead be allowed to rest.

Perhaps *I* believe.

Something is irritating the skin of my hand. It forces me to avert my gaze from the tower. A pinprick of blood turns to a globule. With a slap of my other hand, I squash the blood-sucking insect. It's a close and humid night but perhaps I'd better move away from the cabin window as the midges are feasting.

Tonight, I'll not concern myself with the Zoroastrian priests and their acolytes, but dream about my beautiful model Zoë instead. (Well, I'm calling her that, she hasn't actually told me her name, but she doesn't seem to mind.) Perhaps she will allow me to paint her nakedness tomorrow.

If I can persuade her.

Well, it *is* art.

***

I had another good session with Zoë today. She was there when I arrived in the late afternoon as we had arranged, and she sat by the tree near the barrow as before.

I wanted to tell her all about the tower. I think she was genuinely interested although it's hard to say because she just continued to stare at me with that oh so reassuring smile of hers. She's very obliging and never complains.

But as the afternoon wore on, the oppressive heat began to take its toll. It was hard going, and it was even beginning to show on Zoë's face … the smile seemed a little forced and her eyes dulled, as though she was losing interest in me and our tryst. Flies and midges buzzed and danced in the air and settled on her forehead. They crawled into her dark locks of hair, which no longer shone in the dappled sunlight.

A worm plopped onto her exposed breast, and was sliding down her flesh. It was hiding in the dirt and grass, I expect. But she did not flinch or move. I suppose she was too tired or lethargic to protest. I approached her, concerned over her discomfort, and at first I thought I saw her smile broaden. For a moment my heart sang, but as I drew closer, I realised it was because the lips had wizened away along with most of her face; the flickering sunrays, so deceitful and mischievous, acting as a trickster, alas.

It was only to be expected.

I gathered her clothes and placed them in the backpack I had found on my first day, which was hidden among the ash trees on the hummock. I presume the bag belonged to her; she must have been a hiker who had strayed, or was abducted from the nearby canal towpath.

Not that it really matters.

***

One more day with her, I think.

It's close and humid again tonight, but before I left her by the tree I heard a slight chill breeze sigh through the boughs. I imagined it sounded like the softness of her voice that I'd never heard and it made me sad. I covered her nakedness with some fallen leaves and bracken, just in case she caught a chill.

Besides, I wouldn't want any passers-by to see us like this; they might think I'm weird or something.

Tonight, when the tower appears on the hill again, I wonder if I'll see Zoë hanging there.

Lost Souls

There is a small town on the Pembrokeshire coast called Seaby and it nestles below the cliff path along the rugged shoreline.

There is something rather charming about the scatter of beach huts and surfers along the stretches of sand, and the souvenir stalls, cafés and bookshops that display their wares among the steep and narrow alleyways. It is quite unspoilt; there are no amusement arcades, fair grounds or noisy motorcycles to disturb the quiet sleepiness of the town.

My wife and I were particularly fond of this quiet idyll. When I think of her, I see her on the rocky, windswept beach, standing beside her easel, working with her pallet and paintbrush. I can still hear the sound of the gulls and smell the surf; the vivid mood still lingers within me. It's as if she became a part of the watercolours she so lovingly created - I can envision her among the vistas of colour; standing, walking, smiling with joy; a splash of yellow capturing the sunlight on her face. Her soul resided in those paintings.

On the western edge of the town, you can walk along a quiet, cobblestoned alleyway that leads down a steep slope, and on the corner, where the row of seafront buildings begin, you will find Saint Govan's Inn, a cosy and inviting restaurant, fronting the harbour. The latticed, Georgian style bay windows are reminiscent of the stern of an old galleon ship, and on display, amid drapes of old mariner rope and riggings, there are ornaments and curios: table lamps, an array of Art Nouveau, candlesticks and figurines, trinkets, seashells, snuff boxes, old coins, and silverware.

I think it was in that restaurant, quite a few years ago, that all this began. Quite fitting really; we had spent many a cosy tryst there, hands entwined, hearts, minds and souls as one … so if we were ever going to repair the damage and rekindle our love, then this was the place to do it. We had booked a table for supper, and were fortunate to be seated in an alcove by the window filled with a myriad of baubles and treasures. It overlooked the harbour.

I remember studying Cynthia's expression. She looked tired and fraught in spite of our weekend away. I forced a smile of sort, feigning kindness; she was, after all, trying so hard. I squeezed her hand in an effort to reassure her yet again. Yes, I still loved her, but until I could bring myself to forgive her for what she'd done, I just couldn't see her in the same light anymore.

As we ate our meal she started to talk … to open up, but I'm afraid my mind was wandering. Perhaps I had given up trying to save the situation by then; my heart and soul just wasn't in it. She began with her usual outpouring of remorse, and said something about us leaving England and starting afresh elsewhere – Paris or Vienna, maybe. I could relocate with the Company, and she could start painting again; then we could put the past behind us. It washed over me; I was gazing absently out of the window into the night, listening to the gentle tinkling of the boats' moorings and watching their lights sway from the incoming tide.

… Until, that is, I caught a movement amid the ornaments and decorative rigging in the window, revealed by the cosy glow from the elegant lamps; a shimmy among the shadows and crevices between the many Art Deco bronze figurines - equestrian, mariners, fish - something craving my attention. Finally, I spotted her - the mermaid - nestling among the cowries and pebbles. The light caught her eyes as she looked and smiled at me invitingly.

There was nothing to cover her nakedness, save for her wavy hair shielding her breasts. She lay on her belly with her torso raised and resting on her elbows. Yet to me she was beautiful and serene; brought to life within the dim, shadowy glow. I was drawn to the curve of her hips, and her scaly, tapering fish-tail waving playfully in the air. So enchanting, so alluring.

Yes, a playful coquette … craving attention. It's funny, I'd never noticed her before, but now I was loath to avert my gaze.

"She's quite eye-catching isn't she?" Cynthia's voice had broken the spell, "Come on, let's go for a stroll along the quay."

We left the restaurant and began our little walk. There was a chill breeze blowing over the harbour;

the boats bobbed agitatedly in the swell, and the bells on their moorings jangled more excitedly. Cynthia shivered, and hooked her arm round mine as much to draw my attention than stave off the cold.

"We go home in a couple of days ... will you have decided by then?" She spoke in that nervous, insecure way – I'd grown to hate that.

"I don't know, Cyn. It's best not to pressure me. If only I could get the feeling of betrayal out of my head, we could move on."

"But I want us to be together forever. It's still the same me ... the woman you married .... I just felt bored ... just for a moment. He promised me so much."

But that was the trouble; I no longer saw her as 'the same me'. Yes, I maintained a deep affection for her but the trouble was, not as a wife. I thought back to that day... the day I caught them in bed; *our* bed. And I could no longer look at her nakedness as loving and tender; now it was vile and cheap. It may as well have been putrid and rotten, for at that moment, I actually wished that she would die. I don't know who died that day, her or me.

I unhooked her from me and turned to face her. Her dark, curled locks of hair danced across her cheek in the breeze, and the lights of the harbour reflected in her tears.

"Why don't you make love to me anymore?" She stuttered betwixt the sobbing.

"I want to ... I wish we could go back to how it was."

"We can." She smiled hopelessly, and pulled me closer to her as we recommenced our saunter.

"I'll begin painting again and find another gallery to work for … we'll leave this behind. I'll find a new agent … not him … and all will be well, you'll see."

***

The next morning we resolved to do separate things; take a little time out alone. Cynthia had decided to explore the gift shops and art galleries offering their wares among the narrow thoroughfares, so I took a stroll along the cliff paths to the west of the town. The winds were strengthening, but the sun splashed its rays over sea and land, colouring the rolling thunderclouds an incandescent purple. The grasses and heathlands on the cliff tops were bathed with golden, autumnal sheens.

I fought against the gusts, the chill causing my eyes to water, and every now and then I stole a glance over the scarp and to the beaches and coves. The sheer drop made me giddy. Far below, a man was struggling in vain to control his kite; it soared into the sky, its wires dragging him across the sand. Two boys ducked and weaved around him in wild exhilaration, their distant cries of excitement carried by the wind.

I surveyed the vista - the crashing seas with its blues and greys, the olive greens of the high plateaux pocked with the shadows of the scudding clouds - and raised my face to the sky. This desolate expanse was truly a magnificent place to be on such a day and it warmed and comforted me. I felt that I could walk for miles without meeting a living soul. I was alone, but not lonely.

The path weaved between each inlet on each successive peninsular, and I lost all track of time, until that is, I began to tire and slow. I crouched by the edge and gazed into the cove and beach below. It was so isolated, remote and deserted, but there, the sun shone bright and uninterrupted on the golden, untainted sand. I shuffled partway down the incline – as far as I dare – and nestled on a grassy ledge, basking in the warmth of the sun, and sheltering from the wind. My thoughts mingled with the cacophony of sea spray and gulls. Perhaps I fell asleep.

That was when I noticed her. A woman had emerged from the rocks hidden beneath me, her dark hair and the tails of her overcoat flapping in the whipping air-current. As she strode across the shore, two labradors, as black in the sun's bright as her figure, were kicking the sand around her. They barked excitedly and battled against the waves thrusting at their heels.

I can't explain why, but she fascinated me. She was staring at the sea – to the distant horizon. Eventually she walked on. I watched her until she disappeared behind a rocky crag, and I lost sight of her.

My heart sank; I had wanted to know more about her. Maybe she would suddenly emerge on to the clifftop from a path nearby if she had left the beach, but it was hard to tell – the terrain and the light may have been playing tricks on me.

A glance at my watch brought me back; it was time to meet Cynthia at Saint Govan's for our evening meal.

As I descended the cobbles towards the inn, I paused by the window, and searched for my trinket mermaid. Where was she? Amid the clutter of objets d'art, she was difficult to spot. *Where was she?* I became anxious. Did I imagine her?

There ... hiding in the shadows cast by the lamplight. I could see her fishy tail and flowing mane, but her head was turned and her face hidden as though she was staring at the empty table and waiting for me.

"Hello." Cynthia's call jolted me. "Shall we go in?"

I made sure that we were seated as we were the night before. Within moments of our settling, my beautiful mermaid greeted me with her beckoning smile; her eyes inviting, her body bathed in the warm glow of the light. Joy!

When the waitress came over to take our order, I found myself asking about the figurine.

"Ah, the siren of the sea!" she said in a mocking tone. "She's born from solid bronze; it's an original, not a cast or a copy. The restaurant owner acquired it on one of his travels; Spain I think."

She gestured at the whole display. "He picks up these knick-knacks from around the world."

I sighed. I wanted to steal my paramour away.

***

But I'm reminiscing over events that occurred long ago. I cannot recall what Cynthia and I talked about on our last evening together. Nothing much I expect, as that all that needed to be said had been said.

The following morning, I paid a visit to the small museum. It's located at the end of a pathway that leads up to the cliff edge, away from the town. I remember gazing at the boats in the harbour as I climbed the steep cobbles as well as the quaint lantern street lamps … I really didn't want to leave there. I didn't want to go home anymore.

The main story the museum boasts, is that of the botched French invasion that occurred there in 1797, when some fourteen hundred soldiers, sailors and convicts – an undisciplined, unruly mob – led by an American colonel, one William Tate, landed ashore in nearby Fishguard. It all went awry when, in a drunken state, they were fooled into surrendering to the local women who were dressed in traditional red cloaks; they mistook them for British grenadiers. The women were hailed as heroes.

However, a small group of the mariners escaped by boat, but met their demise when they were washed ashore among the rocks near Seaby, and drowned. No-one really knew why they strayed so close to the shore, except that is, for the locals. "Sirens," they declared, "The call of the sirens … to lay claim on their souls."

But, I digress. I headed back to the hotel around mid-morning to meet Cynthia, but she was gone. A note had been carefully placed on the bureau in our room. It read:

"I have decided to return early, and catch the next train.

When I'm home, I will pack a few belongings, and stay with my sister in Paris. She and André will look after me.

I am so sorry how things have turned out, and I hope you will eventually come to forgive me.

All my Love,

Cyn -xx-"

I don't think I've seen her since. I felt numb and empty. Something that had been dying inside me had drawn its final breath; all those years of companionship and belonging … that part of my life had gone. As with a dying elderly loved one finally released from pain, I felt no grief – just emptiness.

Perhaps I should have followed her, but instead, I found myself returning to my lonely vigil on the windswept precipice, and staring at the same remote, sandy cove below as before.

I'm not sure how long I waited – perhaps a mere blink of an eye – but the woman reappeared; the same purposeful stride, the same wind tossed hair.

This time, I had to approach her. I walked agitatedly back and forth along the cliff edge, searching for a pathway down to the cove. At last I found one. It seemed to veer off in the wrong direction, but I surmised that eventually, it would wind its way to sea level. The path was slippery and dangerous as it zigzagged, and twice in my haste, I nearly lost my footing. But I kept telling myself that the approach must be passable, otherwise, how had *she* got down there?

As I descended, the wind dropped, barred by the sheltering rock face, and the crash of the surf became hollow and hushed. I was relieved to set my foot on the dry, dusty sand.

I looked in every direction anxiously, fearing I was too late and she'd disappeared again. There, over yonder, the distant black figure continued her journey, now close to the water's edge. I crossed the dune hurriedly, the spray and the spittle of the breakers soaking me. I *had* to catch up with her, but the waves and the gathering shingle made my strides heavy; I would have to quicken my pace.

How would I greet her? What would she think? I had no wish to alarm her. I would conjure a story and say that I wanted to warn her about the incoming tide, and that if she was not careful, she might be cut off since there was no quick escape up the ridge.

As I approached, I realised she was searching for something. But I was tiring; my legs were aching, my breathing laboured, and the noise and ferocity of the waves, together with the sticky sand clogging my feet were confounding me. I was soaked through, stressed, disoriented.

She must have halted … she must have. Suddenly, she was upon me, her face looming. She didn't seem surprised by my presence; it was almost as if she was expecting me.

"My dogs are missing. They've disappeared, and I fear for them."

I was mesmerised at the way her large sea-green eyes beneath the dark lashes were studying me; her fresh, pale complexion and high cheekbones were strikingly beautiful, as was her hair undulating in the breeze, and flowing to her hips. It was strange – almost seductive – and added to my feeling that her youthful appearance belied her years. She exuded an air of great wisdom and knowledge.

"I'll … I'll help you look for them." Those were my clumsy, stammering words.

He full lips matched the colour of her eyes, and betrayed the faintest of smiles. She knew I was under her spell.

She continued her walk. I followed. We never spoke; the crash of the waves and gulls' cry drowned any hope of dialogue.

We were heading inland, away from the incoming surf, and towards a cave entrance, out of which the angry, rolling sea boiled and spewed. The din was overwhelming. The sand gave way to shale and pebbles, making my strides heavy and clumsy. The water's swell formed a pool of inky blackness at the cavern's maw, and I squinted into the gaping darkness within to try and determine its size – how far it stretched inside the cliff wall.

She halted at its mouth, where the eddying tide swirled at our feet. "I knew you would come," she said, "I made it my will."

I studied her face, her expression, and frowned. I thought about the mermaid.

She spoke as she stared at me. "It is here where

the doomed French seafarers were washed ashore and drowned when their boat capsized. Lost souls … but you know of this from the museum."

I nodded meekly.

Her half-smile reappeared. "They were lured into these caves by a beautiful woman crying and calling to them, but of course it was a phantom – a siren consigning them to a watery grave – so the legend goes …. Do you believe in legends?"

She lowered her voice and her smile dropped. "Sometimes you can hear their wails and cries … listen!"

It was odd, but the whining wind from the cave mouth seemed to mimic a distant voice calling; a woman's cry … and of men's howls of despair … somewhere in the distance.

I shivered.

She turned away again and continued onward along a narrow, slippery ledge into the cave. I had to follow, the compulsion was too great. As soon as I entered the pitch, the sun's rays were extinguished. My eyes couldn't adjust; my body tensed. I was terrified that I would lose my footing and plunge into the black, heaving swell below me, and I clung to any piece of jutting rock available. I was sheltered from the wind, but the air was oppressive – my senses were assaulted by the stench of dampness and rotting seaweed.

She was just inches from my touch, and still with her back to me, but, oh, how her exquisite, silky hair, cascaded to her waist … it was entrancing. I wanted her.

My recollections after that are so vivid … they linger.

She stopped abruptly, her body inert, and with her back to me, *still.* I gazed forlornly in the direction I'd come – towards the light. The dazzling sun was no more than a remote and feeble patch emanating from the cave entrance. The intoxicating odour of the lapping, sable water, had made me light-headed and giddy.

Giddy with desire.

I wrapped my arm round her waist and stroked her hair. She turned at – last – and as I cupped my palm on her cheek, she pressed her lips to mine. I swear I could hear her soft, caressing sigh in my ear, but it was so dark and murky …

… And, with her face so close to mine, I saw the horror within the time it took for a single beat of my heart: The soulless, hollow eye-sockets … and cheeks of deathly white, cold, hard and clammy, pressing against my cheek. And the stench from her breath – like rotting algae hissing through putrid, yellow, rotten teeth. It caused me to gag.

I recoiled and must have lost my balance and slipped, because the ice-cold water hit me like a sledge-hammer. I was blind, I was gasping for breath, my limbs flailing.

And something, was tugging at my legs, pulling me down … down.

Bitter, salty water bubbling and boiling in my ears and down my throat … so cold … so cold … so black.

… And then a sharp stab of pain in my chest; my lungs were bursting, and … and, I must have blacked out; I remember nothing after that.

***

I am unable to recollect much about my subsequent visits to Seaby, though I do recall returning to Saint Govan's Inn. My mermaid is no longer there.

That is sad.

Same too goes for the woman on the beach. I keep returning to that lonely hinterland, day after day, year after year, but she hasn't reappeared. I wait there on the sands, and eventually wander over to the cave. People pass me by, but they ignore me. It's as though I'm invisible; strange that.

Still, as time passes, I cannot recall going anywhere else, or seeing *anybody*. My soul belongs on that windswept shore.

As for my heart, well, that belongs with the woman who called me there.

Stourhead, Wiltshire

The beautiful, atmospheric gardens of Stourhead in Wiltshire and the monuments therein known as "The Obelisk" and "King Alfred's Tower", inspired me to write this and another story. I'm unaware of any ghosts or hauntings there, but if one was fortunate enough to wander alone among the gardens, parkland and follies on a sunny winter's day, or just before the sun goes down, the imagination would surely kindle.

And for the author in particular, since penning "The Obelisk" and "The Wildess", on subsequent visits, there have been two occasions where life has imitated art; curious indeed.

The Obelisk

Billy wished it could always be like this as he lay in bed with the girl of his dreams snuggling up to him. As the warmth of the duvet and the silky feel of her naked body closed round him, her lips pressed on his cheek and it tickled. She purred, her lips parted and emitted a tiny chuckle.

Flickering shades of sapphirine bathed her face and breast, and caused him to turn his starry gaze to the source of the light in the far corner of the room; it shimmered like a ghost.

"Look – the computer's rebooting. I must have left the monitor on – see how it glows."

"Mmm, leave it'." She breathed in his ear as her hand moved playfully on his chest.

"No, it's strange. I wonder what those messages are, flashing across the screen?"

He unhooked the fleshy thigh straddling his hips and slid from the cosiness of the duvet, the sudden cold chilling his nakedness. He threw her a glance, regretting his act when he heard the sigh and groan emanating from the warm bundle he'd left behind. She'd buried herself out of sight, into the comfort of the bed.

He watched the monitor as it flickered and whirred, drawn to the incomprehensible chatter of computer gobbledegook manifesting before him, too fast for him to read. Why did it insist on doing that? What was the point?

Rebooting the mother board…

Searching file directories…

Obtaining profiles…

The Obelisk…

I love you.

What?

He shook his head. Did it really say that?

A fleeting moment, and the message was gone. He must have imagined it.

Yes, that was it, his mind was working overtime as all restless minds do when alone in the dead of night. Do a thousand messages flash through your brain and form a story? An account of impossible events and imaginings? Was that what the computer was doing? Recollecting, taking stock … dreaming? He wondered what happened to your brain when you dreamed. Was it taking stock, reorganising, rebooting in the same way as the thing in front of him?

Another playful giggle sounded in the dark, but he couldn't detect any stirrings, or rustling of sheets when he peered over his shoulder and into the darkness.

"Mmm … come back to bed, Billy, it's cold."

"In a minute, Pippa …"

The light from the monitor continued to flash across the room like a silent display of lightning; teasing moments, illuminating her silky hair upon her shoulder and the gossamer sheen of her flesh, which, in between the bursts, was cast in the darkened, ice blue hues of the night. Yet still her expression stayed hidden; a mask of grey. There were no features; even her cobalt, inviting lips that a moment ago pressed so close to his, eluded him. No more nestling of hips and limbs, nor playful purring; no more dreamy sighs. Perhaps she had fallen asleep. An awful feeling of insecurity imbued him.

Suddenly the dancing blue light stopped and the room turned still and black; the blue snuffed out. He swivelled on the chair to face the monitor again. A dazzling radiance of green and red assaulted his eyes.

The Christmas party.

A picture he'd taken at the annual office gathering, glowed.

The screen had frozen. Maybe the file was corrupt or something. Maybe that was the reason the computer was behaving the way it was.

A dozen faces stared back at him in drunken revelry from round a table, amidst the streamers, party poppers, wine bottles and half eaten mince pies, their expressions suspended in time, yet still sentient by the static effulgence of the pixels. Daniel the youth, drunk as always, face looming at the camera, and with his latest unsuspecting female clinging at his arm. On the opposite side, the lads, all three of them with lob sided paper hats, glasses raised, and, no doubt, singing out of key.

And there, beside them, was Marsha … lovely Marsha; the bright verdant and reds from the Christmas tree and tinsel framing her form, and her visage glowing radiant from the blur of the log fire in the background.

Ah yes, the Christmas party …

He hadn't wanted to go of course…well he wasn't much of a party animal really.

"C'mon, Billy, have some fun, let your hair down. Have a drink or two; we'll sort out a lift for you," they all said.

"Yes, but I'm on my own … no-one to talk to. 'Billy No-Mates', that's me."

"Don't worry about that. Marsha will be going. She *wants* you to come."

"Oh … right."

Weeks later the lift was arranged.

"Who's giving me a lift?"

"Marsha. She and her husband say that you can hitch a ride on the back seat."

Oh, God! Of all the people that were going, it had to be her!

Of course, he had done his best to stay unnoticed during the revelries, especially from Marsha – he'd have died if she had actually found time to talk to him, or, perish the thought, she had asked him to *dance*. But then he was expert at that sort of thing - hiding away that is; avoiding the limelight.

The hall - the venue - formed part of Sulcroft Manor, and was a lovely setting, he couldn't deny that. It was sumptuously adorned with the usual festive decorations, the centrepiece of which was a huge Christmas tree next to a roaring log fire in the stone hearth. Chandeliers and baubles glittered by the glow of the fairy lights. The manor and the extensive grounds were landscaped in keeping with its grand status dating from its Georgian heyday.

But Billy had no time to appreciate any of that. The chamber was filled with tables crammed with party-goers, but at least the people next to him were from his own circle, and they were amiable enough. All he had to do was nod and smile and listen, and take comfort that with the ever increasing din of the music, conversation no longer mattered.

He drew closer to the screen, his curiosity inflamed. Odd that - he couldn't recall Marsha being at the opposite side of the table at all; he assumed that she was lost to him somewhere in the sea of tables and bodies across the hall … or dancing with her newly wed and their cronies. She couldn't possibly be interested in him, but even so he wished she didn't behave the way she did - not with them.

Yet there she was on the image … looking directly at him.

Then when the wine had flowed, and the dance music throbbed, he had retreated to the bar in time honoured fashion, and continued to nod and smile at the few people he knew as they passed by for refills. Daniel, of course, appeared on more than one occasion.

The stark flashing of the monitor replaced the festive colours, and shook him into bleary-eyed alertness again. The computer had started to reboot once more, obviously having failed at whatever it was trying to do, and resumed its fleeting, ephemeral blather.

He shivered and rubbed the palms of his hands on his naked shoulders. His nose tingled with the cold and he noticed frost crystals on the window glistening blue by the light. He reached for his gown tossed on the bare floorboards and covered himself.

Ah yes … frost.

His mind, like the machine, continued to recall, *to reboot …*

Daniel eyed Billy while simultaneously attempting to negotiate the stool at the bar next to him. His efforts were clumsy, his eyes were glazed and his speech slurred. "Hey, Billy! Me and Daisy are going for a stroll in the grounds. There's a circular walk and hidey-holes and monuments and things. It'll be a right lark. Want to come?"

"What, in the frost and chill of night?"

But he gazed warily at the dance floor. The revellers were preparing for the hokey cokey… and gesturing at him! He drained his glass. Maybe Daniel wasn't such a bad lad after all.

They pushed through the noisy crowd and wandered on to the parterre.

The whirring of the computer stopped again and in the silence, another image - a strange, weatherworn face - leered at him from the screen. A face of stone.

The satyr.

Half man, half beast, the creature had the torso of Hercules, but the legs and hooves of a mythical being, and a horned head akin to the devil. It stared down at him from its plinth on the steps of the parterre with wide, nocturnal eyes and with a grotesque leer. It stood upright and poised, ready to pounce. The lichen and detritus that choked the crumbling stone did nothing to conceal its malevolence or the sense that it seemed somehow alive.

A bright moon, its radiating hues mimicking the monitor, bathed the garden in icy cerulean shades, and lit the rime coating the ground. Daniel's expression was luminant, but his lips were cobalt blue in the cold as he prattled with the vapour from his breath puffing into the air.

"The terraces lead down the slope, and there are hidden pathways among the woods surrounding the lake. On the way there are all sorts of surprises lurking in corners and around each bend…you know, statues, follies and so on."

He wavered and swayed until he dropped his glass. He sniggered as it smashed to pieces; they sparkled like frost crystals.

"Yes, I'm well aware Daniel, my dad used to take me here when I was small."

Billy looked up at the leering satyr.

Daniel remained unperturbed. "Marsha and a few others have gone ahead of us; they're going to the temple of Apollo at the far side of the lake."

"Marsha! She's out here too? I thought she'd be dancing the night away."

Daniel nudged him drunkenly; " All the more reason for our s'cursion then?"

A small, wiry female appeared from the French windows, and peered at them nervously.

" Are we going into the garden then, Danny?"

"Yes, Daisy. C'mon, it'll be a lark."

They ambled down the pathway and past the fountain, heading towards the woodland and the encroaching darkness beyond, the drink shielding them from the numbing raw. Billy glanced behind him at the diminishing festive lights and gaiety, before it was snuffed out by the bough of a tree. The satyr had absconded too, as if it had sneaked off furtively into the night – a trick of the moonlight and shadows, Billy supposed.

The dark closed in on them, leaving only the sparkling frost to illuminate their faces and puffing breaths as they walked down the wooded trackway. Daniel eyed Daisy's clumsy attempts to master her high heels. As she wobbled and swaggered he smirked and turned his attention to Billy. "So you know a bit about the place then?"

"The landscape garden yes … built by an

eccentric in the style of Capability Brown."

The name was lost on Billy's companions but he continued nevertheless. "Took him all his life it did, and it sent him quite mad apparently. He was trying to achieve some kind of immortality so they say, and they reckon that his ghost lives on in the trees and the statues … oh, and the obelisk, that's where he's buried. I've never been there; it's off the beaten track and away from the lakeside. It's supposed to loom at you from the summit of a pathway that cuts through one of the many avenues of trees – if you can find which one."

They arrived at a quadrangle, enclosed and sealed by clipped hedgerows, and Daisy made for the stone bench in the corner. She grimaced and clasped at her broken high heel, shivering, her mood sullen. "This is a stupid, rotten idea, Danny—"

Her whingeing was cut short by her shriek. She pointed to a figure staring at them from the blackness of the opposite corner.

Then Billy realised; he approached the statue and tapped the nude sculpture on the shoulder. It didn't respond of course but just met him with a soulless smile.

Billy pondered. "Hmm, the same as all the other statues lurking around. I wonder who she's supposed to be … Venus, Daphne, Rhea? Trapped for all eternity … or at least until her weather-beaten, lichen encrusted body decays and crumbles away. Some immortality – see how she stares at us with an impassive, dead expression … her eyes are devoid of pupils."

But such notions were beyond Daisy. After making sure the heel was secure again, she muttered incomprehensibly, and stomped off in the direction they came.

Daniel chuckled. "I suppose I'll have to go after her; see if you can find Marsha."

They disappeared into the darkness, staggering, his laughter in time to her protestations; their cackle fading in the ether. Billy wondered just how long Daniel would hang on to that particular catch.

The cold night air had sobered him; that and the creeping dark. He was alone; something he'd always known. He looked back at the eerie, ghost like, figure of the statue, shining white in the moon. His own remark about the spirit of the dead architect living on inside every shadow and recess, every tree and monument, designed to impress and scare, now rebounded on him.

The monitor flickered again. He turned towards the bed. Pippa lay still, and wrapped in the duvet; her shape obscured in the gloom. And so silent; no more playful sounds. She *must* have fallen asleep, but he wasn't sure. He listened for the rhythmic sighs of her breathing. Nothing. A tear formed in his eye as he thought how lucky he had been to find her there at the obelisk.

The obelisk…

There it was, resplendent on the monitor screen. He remembered.

The tall, narrow column stood some sixty feet

high and bore down from the end of a gently rising boulevard of manicured grass, coated in rime, and on either side, a dense row of firs walled him in. A breeze rustled through the foliage and boughs; the trees were whispering conspiratorially, it seemed. Perhaps the spirit of a madman did indeed dwell among them – especially if his body was lying under the obelisk …

He looked at the towering pillar ahead of him. It gleamed bright against the jet blackness of the sky from which no stars shone.

The breeze whipped up angrily. The spirit was awakening; becoming agitated.

Such were Billy's thoughts there alone in the darkness, with the cold confusing him and making him sleepy …very sleepy.

Marsha was beside him. He couldn't recall how he had found her, but they were walking towards the obelisk, which loomed ever larger and imposing. She prattled about how she had lost the others. Perhaps they'd abandoned her. Well it served her right, for this wasn't how he'd hoped she would be. She was moody and irritable. She complained, she grizzled … her attitude made her rather shallow. Disappointing. Maybe she was not his heart's desire after all.

Then the madness began …

A buzzing noise sounded in Billy's ears. It whined and whistled, low-pitched and high. It was all around them.

She halted abruptly and barged into Billy. She

shrieked, staggering, her arms flailing. She clutched her face and tore at her hair, and scratched and clawed her eyes and throat.

"What the ***hell*** is it? Get it ***off*** of me!" She screamed, panic-stricken.

She fell to her knees and continued to maul her head as she cursed and squealed.

Billy stood helpless. "Some sort of nocturnal insect … a mosquito I reckon."

"It's stinging me … ***help me, it's biting at me.***" Her indignation had turned to sobs.

Then, just as suddenly, it stopped. Her sobbing ceased, and she held her breath …. She yowled. Her features were ashen in the moonlight, as, still on her knees, she pointed her finger at something behind him. Her eyes were wide and terror-stricken, and her mouth gaping. But the scream choked in her throat. Something brushed Billy's cheek; the touch of a wispy spider's web. A face – a man, old, deathly white with manic eyes staring – pressed against his. Then it was gone in a heartbeat. He thought he glimpsed a figure with a black cape running away from them into the trees and towards the obelisk.

Still whimpering, she held out her hand for Billy to help her. Her hair was bedraggled and mascara ran down her cheeks. Mud stained the trails of her party dress and stockings, and her face, anaemic and wan, was pin-pricked with punctures of blood.

Billy was shaken – the old man's stare, so horrible, manifesting from out of the dark – but the thing that stung more was her lack of concern for *his* well-being.

She brushed herself down uselessly, cursing her dress, the dirt, her surrounds, and *him*.

"Stupid party, stupid bloody place, ***ugh!*** I'm going back now, and I don't care how long it takes. You - all of you - can go hang for all I care!" Her shrill voice echoed emptily across the blackened valley as she stomped off down the pathway … before slipping down onto the hoarfrost. "Help me, I'm hurt." She grimaced, clutching her buttock.

Billy didn't care. He caught a reflection from the top of the tower and it spurred him on towards the edifice; Marsha no longer mattered.

His mind barely registered her final scream of terror - a distant, piercing wail at the far end of the slope - and the peculiar gurgling and belching noise that ensued, because an angry wind had whipped up and was rustling the firs. It whistled and moaned in his ears - noises akin to whispers and sighs - and shadows danced from the corner of his eye. The whole canopy writhed agitatedly, brought to life by an unholy revocation.

But he was glad he continued onwards - glad because of Pippa.

Softly driven footsteps - hooves, perhaps - pattered behind him from the direction of Marsha's awful, dying scream. As he drew closer, he noticed the sculptured stone figures along the broad and lofty plinth of the obelisk - he was certain they weren't there before. All wore that same vacant, imprisoned stare as the statue in the valley - permanent and frozen; prisoners within the nocturne. At the top of the column, a jewel twinkled in the moon.

He had arrived. The trees and the boulevard were behind him, and he was out in the open. The wind and the whispers that conspired in the dark had ceased and the night air was still again.

He circled the base of the obelisk. Patterns resembling hieroglyphs glistened in the frost like black beads. The cylindrical column towered into the sky, and on top a disc of gold gleamed – the source of the alluring jewel. Wavy spikes resembling sunrays radiated from its centre, where a face, another that leered and grinned, was carved onto the disc. It made no sense at all. He stepped back, taking it in: this was no war memorial; the whole thing seemed to mock him. Sun gods? Hieroglyphs? Or merely a homage to the insane?

Something moved furtively from the shadows. To turn and run like Marsha was not an option. No, best to confront this madness all around him head on – be defiant and show that he was unafraid. He fooled himself into believing that Daniel had reappeared with yet another churlish prank. He turned the corner of the block just in time to catch the hooves of the running satyr disappear round the far side.

"Hello."

The voice made him start. A young woman stepped out from where it had vanished.

"I'm sorry, I should have revealed my presence before calling out. I didn't mean to startle you. I'm Pippa."

The elfin figure approached him, but the wide gleaming eyes were dark as cobalt blue, and matched the lips that formed a disarming, seductive smile. They contrasted with her waxen skin shining in the pale light. Her sudden appearance beguiled him.

"I think these satyrs are everywhere" she said, reading his thoughts. "I think the architect positioned them in such a way as to make you believe that the same one follows you as you meander through the landscape of the garden … a naughty imp that's up to no good."

The light in her eyes glinted in the frost, and the moon revealed a more furtive smile.

"You must have come up here with the others … for a lark?" he ventured, his voice betraying his uncertainty.

No answer; her smile broadened, then she buried her face in the collar of her overcoat. "It's getting cold. We should go back."

She linked her arm in his and he no longer felt alone. His fear dissolved like his breath in the icy air; this was meant to be – kismet. He paid no heed to Marsha's splayed corpse – to the dried rivulets of mascara stained tears that ran from its staring eyes and streaked across the pallid cheeks – and stepped over it without a passing thought.

He ventured a question. "It's funny, I can't remember seeing you at the party?"

"Oh, I've been there all the time. I was hoping that you would notice me … you see, I'm not keen on parties really; I suppose I'm a bit shy."

He couldn't believe his luck. He'd found his soul mate; he hadn't thought that possible.

She nestled her head on his shoulder and the gossamer feel of her hair and the warmth of her skin brushed against the coldness of his. It felt so good.

She tilted her face towards him. "So do *you* think that the spirit of the architect lives on through the landscape he created? That is … in the statues, the temples and follies, and the trees he planted?"

This was too good to be true. It was as though she were reading his mind, as if she'd known him forever.

She continued, not needing an answer. "His body lies under the obelisk, but you already know that. He can manifest whenever he chooses and his malevolent ghost has the power to possess many things, living or artificial." She clung on to his sleeve. "It's scary and insane, but exciting too."

She paused, deep in thought, frowning. "Or it can take on a living form of its own … a person appearing out of nowhere." She nodded at that and tightened her hug.

A form of its own.

Those were her words. Billy sat back from the monitor. A passing remark, but he realised its significance now…

He recalled how they spoke of many things as they wound their way arm in arm, back to the parterre and Sulcroft Manor. They talked at length, theorising that when our bodies and brains die, our minds move on, but the images and events associated with emotion and trauma can be left imprinted in objects – stone, in particular – and are waiting to be 'played back' like a video by a receptive person.

… Or a computer – yes, he remembered that was *his* suggestion. Well it's just a collection of memory banks isn't it? As with a dream, a computer recalls, stores, and plays back – the perfect device for such a psychic imprint to reside.

His thoughts raced and a sense of unease began to seep into Billy's consciousness as he looked at the screen before him. The files were backing up and storing, and flashing random phrases; the same as how a mind experiences a dream.

A form of its own.

Too good to be true.

Then came the days of bliss after the party – a party he would not have missed for the world. They were never apart. "I love you so very much" she would say to him. It was like a dream. She was so perfect and she strived to please him in any way he could imagine.

And so to this very night, they had made love … and it was every bit as divine as he could hope for. Her sensual, warm body yielded to him, and her heart and soul were so loving and comforting. Her caresses and sighs of devotion told him that she did indeed mean what she had said: "I love you so much." She uttered the words so many times.

… So why then, was he sitting in the dark and the chill, staring into the mesmeric light of a computer screen as it flickered useless phrases of gobbledegook, when he could be lying in Pippa's arms?

The image of the obelisk had disappeared and the computer had started to reboot again and spew its strange language

This is a bad argument

You have performed an illegal operation.

He wanted the warmth of Pippa and the bed, so he reached for the power switch.

Warning! All unsaved data will be lost.

Are you sure you want to quit?

The very moment he flicked the switch, a heart-stopping cry of anguish sounded from behind him, and the springs from the mattress cracked. He was certain he saw the shape of her body beneath the covers jerk and twitch.

"Pippa?"

Silence.

"Pippa, are you all right?"

A terrible realisation overwhelmed him. What had he just done?

Too good to be true. Too good to be true.

He walked over to the bed but he could see the shape within was no longer there. He turned on the lamp and pulled back the duvet.

The bed was empty and cold.

Summer's Feast

I feel the need to get away from here. Up sticks, sell up, scarper.

After what has happened …

I can't stop thinking about the woman and the ogre. Freddy Milligan too

I have lived in the tiny village of Lower Pontby for most of my life, and until now, I've always thought of it as home, for here, in this lonely isolated pocket hidden among leafy narrow lanes, the sun always seems to shine. It is a quiet idyll, and on a balmy summer's evening, nothing disturbs the gentle breeze as it rolls through the pasture and cornfields, save for bird song and the drone of the bee. Strange to think of the desolate expanse of the fens lying just to the north.

Ah, Freddy Milligan … that day in the top field by the ridge near Steen's Folly, up across the pasture beyond the old school playground, where we ducked and dived between the thistles and cow pats.

What Milligan didn't know about playing in meadows, secret dens, and boyhood mischief, wasn't worth a jot. He sat next to me in class. I can picture him now: pint-size, scruffy, tie at half-mast, grimy knees poking out from below his short trousers, a runny nose … and when he lifted the lid of his desk, an Aladdin's cave opened up before you. Hidden underneath the dog-eared exercise books were toy soldiers and cars, stray golf balls, playing cards, and a half eaten packet of crisps. Last but not least, there would be a jam jar of murky, smelly pond water, teeming with all sorts of creepy-crawlies - his 'pets' as he would call them. He was a bit of a loner, brought up by his dad, and put himself first, but he was never a bully, and if you ever wanted to lay your hands on anything, he was your man - for the right price of course! And if you really gained his trust, then for twenty pence, he would let you look at his 'nudey pics' - even the one of the woman he swore was Kelly Price's mum. Kelly was the girl who sat at the front of the class. Many's the time 'Grumpy' Grimshaw caught him rummaging in that desk - and not for his times tables - and ordered a clear-out. But Milligan was Milligan; in a day or two all his collected chattels would reappear like magic.

Then there were the newts …

Friday dinner-time, when Grumpy had left the classroom, I happened to mention that I wanted to catch some newts; well, that's what small boys do isn't it?

"I know where you can get some newts, kid … big 'uns too!"

He reached for the smelly jam jar from beneath the desk lid, and thrust it in front of my face. Two hideous beetles were circling in the swirling murk, their antennae twitching, and legs beating in a raged frenzy.

"Great diving beetles … there's a pond up in the top field. Meet me after tea tonight behind the school, and I'll take you there. Oh, and kid … bring your football as well, and we'll have a kick around."

His eyes widened with anticipation as he stared intently at the jam jar. "Take a look what's happened here when we leave class tonight."

The moment the school bell sounded, he threw a furtive glance at Grimshaw and made sure he couldn't see what we were up to. He lifted the desk lid and held the jam jar aloft again.

A satisfied leer morphed on his lips. "See … only one left. They fight to the death, and the loser gets eaten." He shook the jar slightly so as to disturb the brown, flaky sediment of keratin at the bottom – the remains of the defeated combatant.

"Anything dead – its flesh, and blood – gets eaten; absorbed by some other creature."

I grimaced.

"It's nature," he triumphed. "Catch you later, kid."

We set off later on that sticky, humid summer's evening; two mischievous schoolboys on an adventure. I clutched at my fishing net in one hand and a jam jar in the other as we left the school yard for the meadows beyond.

"The pond's in the top field, behind the hedge on the near side," he explained.

But he always kept me on edge, that boy. "What about old Steensy; what if he catches us?"

"Relax, kid, if he chases us with his stick, we'll easily out run him, he's a fogey, an old goat! And anyway, we'll just come back another night."

He forged ahead, kicking my football into the grass and scrub.

It was quite a steep rise, but we got there, and he climbed the last gate into the top field. There, hidden behind the hedgerow, was the pond with all its magical secrets, and, I was sure - newts!

We peered into the water, its still surface darkening by the fading sunset. A disturbance, a ripple; a swirl among the tendrils of weeds. Milligan stooped. "I can see them, our little friends .... Give me yer net."

It was at that point I began to feel afraid, yes, I remember. The comforting, golden orb was sinking, and the reddening sky cast the hedgerow and nearby ruin - Steen's Folly - in shadow. I felt certain we were being watched. That's when I spotted someone creeping about on the ridge.

Yes, afraid, and we were miles from anywhere and cut off; an uneasy sensation. I wanted to go home.

Milligan remained oblivious. "C'mon kid, this is the best time to catch 'em." He snatched the net from my hand and prodded the bubbles rising from the pool.

Suddenly a voice barked, its tone guttural and angry. "You young buggers, I'll 'ave you."

We jumped out of our skins, Milligan's foot sliding on the muddy bank. "Run, it's old Steensy." He dropped the net, and scurried back towards the gate like a startled hare.

Steensy had appeared from nowhere, right in

the middle of the field. I stood rooted to the spot, frozen with fear. It couldn't possibly be who I saw on the ridge. How could he have covered such a distance in so short a time?

Then, I realised there was someone else: a puny, wiry figure of an even older man sitting cross-legged by the stone folly. The memory haunts me – especially now after what's occurred – it's so vivid. His limbs seemed to form part of the branches and twigs of an ugly, squat tree growing from inside the ruins of the folly. He rested his chin in his hands as he stared at me with his beady eyes set behind his hooked nose. Malevolent, evil, *grotesque.*

But my attention soon refocussed on Steens; he was almost upon me, his bloated face red with rage as if the blood vessels were about to burst.

He snarled, and bared his yellow, nicotine stained teeth. "You good for nothing brats. How many times have I told you to stay off my land?"

He raised his stick and I feared he was going to strike, but he pointed to the old man with the passive stare blending among the twigs and crumbling stone. "I'll feed you to my 'Da over there. He'll boil your flesh, he'll grind your bones and he'll throw the left-overs to me pigs ...."

Saliva dribbled from his mouth. I screamed, and spun on my heels, and panic-stricken, *I ran ... I ran like bloody hell.*

I could hear his snarling and panting closing in on me as I leapt over the gate into the lower field, and hoped he'd tire and I'd outrun him; he was on his last legs after all. I caught up with Milligan, who'd stumbled and was lying on his back with his arms and legs flailing around and I thought of the whirling beetles in the jar. I skedaddled; he could take care of himself.

I never hung out with Milligan again – he was a magnet for trouble. I wonder what became of him? Come to think of it, I can't recall seeing him at all following that escapade. Perhaps he and his dad moved away from the district.

No matter.

It's the woman, our mysterious client, that's bothering me, and what has become of *her*; especially when I think of that summer's evening as I drove from the office in town back to Pontby and how relieved and elated I felt. I knew Tom, my business partner and friend, would be pleased too. At last a success story!

I had successfully negotiated the lease of the land surrounding Steen's Folly to a prospective client. It amounted to nothing more than an abandoned barn, dilapidated outbuildings, and neglected scrub and pasture – and that wretched folly on the ridge. It's hard to understand why someone should take an interest, but hey, I wasn't complaining! Neither of us had appreciated that once we had quit the company and set up our own business as estate agents, just how difficult an enterprise we had undertaken.

But as the sun shone, and as I sped along the leafy lanes, I realised part of my contented mood centred on our enigmatic client, Ms. Anna Esquivel, no less, the recluse who had moved to Pontby a few months ago. She had caused tongues to wag in our close-knit community; no-one knew anything about her, or her family ancestry. We assumed that she came from a well-to-do family and may have had a private income – she must have, if she was moving into our exclusive little village. She kept herself to herself, and, on that day when she first graced our office, she described her vocation as 'a writer and artist'. She looked to be around thirty and of Hispanic descent, Tom reckoned, as he ogled her from his desk opposite. She is – *was* – alluring, being so tall, slender, and with long, raven hair. And that slight sheen that highlighted her cheekbones was created by her discerning choice of blusher; a deliberate act, I suspect. Her large brown eyes regarded you with an impassive stare; her aloofness fascinated me – *that and a figure, which you would die for ....*

I could tell she recognised me by the scarcely perceptible glint of her studious, perceptive expression; the day when our paths crossed at the village store.

"I wish to arrange a view of the property as soon as possible, and without any fuss."

"Well, as we both live nearby, I can meet you at the property after work ... say, seven o'clock?" I managed to stammer.

A half-smile formed on her lips; I'm sure she noticed my wistful sigh. Cool and aloof ... that's how I'd describe her.

"Good." She rose from her chair and swaggered

from the office.

Tom grinned as he skulked from behind his computer screen. "Lucky bastard!"

The path to the abandoned outbuildings is not an easy one. I had to cross the graveyard, negotiate a muddy track that lead through the undergrowth, cross the open fields up to the ridge, and make my way down to the barn at the bottom of the slope on the far side.

And all the while the ruined folly and the crouching oak tree next to it brooded on the ridge. That ugly bole of twisted boughs and branches, denuded of foliage, seemed neither dead nor alive. Sounds crazy, but I sensed it was beckoning me. I approached and placed my palm on the trunk. The bark was more russet than brown, and, I'll never forget this, because it felt warm and moist. My hand was coated with thick, dark red, sticky goo. It was almost as if it *were* alive. I swear it trembled when I touched it.

Something scuttled by my feet, but when I looked, nothing was there; perhaps a startled creature had fled from the hollow of the trunk. I recoiled and retreated, quickening my pace, but I paused for a moment. I had to look back and face my fear.

The bole, blackened by the twilight, reminded me of a human figure; a crooked and aged man; its gnarled boughs his limbs, and a protruding twig, a long, hooked nose.

Steensy's dad.

It gave me the creeps, and suddenly an

overwhelming feeling of despair hit me.

I shook my head and tried to snap out of it; this was due to tiredness and worry over the uncertainty surrounding the business. It was affecting me, and so it was important for this meeting to be successful. I walked purposefully in the opposite direction and headed for the barn.

And the scuttling creature? A small dog, I was certain. I could hear its panting and wheezing beside me. It was lost, I expect, and wanted to get away from there as much as I did. True, I never actually saw the mutt, for every time I stopped to look, *it* stopped, and I was met with the familiar silence.

Oh yes, the silence; there was no birdsong. Everywhere was so still, and so *eerie* in the dulling light.

I tottered down the slope on the far side towards the barn – that's where Ms Esquivel would be waiting for me – taking care not to stumble; my mind focussing on the task in hand, and to the imposing building ahead. It resembled a huge, somewhat dilapidated leviathan … and was gloomy and cold inside; musty too, everything smacked of decay. I shivered as the sweat from my exertions began to chill my body. My eyes strained to adjust to the gloom. No-one – Ms Esquivel or anyone – was there to greet me. I called but there was no answer, save for that deafening silence in the stillness. I'd been duped, made a fool of. And I was alone … and spooked.

"Perfect, I'll take it. Attend to the necessary

arrangements."

I jumped as the voice, female, articulate and confident, pierced the ether.

She was watching me from the far end of the building. The dying sun's hues were filtering through the rafters and bathing the outline of her hair and exquisite form encapsulated in her summer dress, with a golden nimbus. It was so beautiful and sultry ... my mouth went dry and my heart thumped.

She walked slowly towards me. I couldn't move. I stood mesmerised by the approaching siren. My solitude was getting to me; that's what it was.

It was difficult to string my sentences together. "Er ...there's the property surveys to discuss, and the land registry—"

She waved her hand dismissively. "I shall have the roof replaced by a skylight of glass. The light is just what I need as this will be the studio where I can paint ... and I won't be disturbed."

She drew close and the seductive half-smile reappeared; perhaps it was the stupid, quizzical look I must have worn. She tilted her head, the pale, diffusing half-light catching her cheekbone and jaw - so feminine - and the dark pools of her eyes. I followed her gaze to the void above. She was taking in the colours of the setting sun, every shifting pattern of its radiance, every shape, every contour and lengthening shadow within our twilight world, until ... her stare reverted to me. God, she was beautiful.

"All that is beauty eventually fades. Everything withers and perishes ... or is destroyed and recycled or consumed. That is why it is important to hunt, and to capture the beauty, in whatever shape or form, and preserve it for posterity, in art."

I thought of Milligan and his beetles.

"So you'll sign the lease then?"

I could have kicked myself. How could I have uttered such a witless remark after so profound a statement?

She answered me with her customary seductive smirk.

I started to blather and stutter in a clumsy attempt to hide my embarrassment. "There's an ancient ruin, that is, a folly … just the other side of the rise … full of myth and legend, very atmospheric … quiet … and there are walks nearby too … perfect for contemplation …. A ruin … in a backdrop against the sky … it might provide you with ideas, that is, inspiration … for your art, I mean."

She raised an eyebrow; her dark eyes widened as she studied me. Her lips parted. "Indeed?"

As I made my return up the slope, I was so fixated on Ms. Esquivel that I paid scant heed to the pattering breaths of the little dog again around my feet.

I returned to the gravel path and the familiar security of the churchyard and village like a love-struck fool, not questioning how she arrived at the barn, or offering to escort her back. I cursed my inadequacy.

But, hey, I'd secured the negotiation on the lease.

***

It was when I started to scrutinise the land registry, sift through the deeds and trace the history and ownership of the property that a mystery began to form.

My fascination for Ms. Esquivel was only equalled by my awakened interest in Steen's Folly. Maybe it was a subconscious act in order to take my mind off the worrying state of our fledgling business – I think our heart and souls were never really in it. Certainly, this was better than dwelling on that, and anyway, that utter sense of despair I felt when I stood in the top field by the ruin played on my mind more than mere business ventures.

Steen's Folly, a small tumbledown tower built from stone, is so named after the farmers who had worked on the land for generations. Locals say it's as old as time itself. It's not a folly in actual fact, but a lookout post built by the Saxons in the eighth century, and used to serve as an early warning when the marauding Vikings crossed the water channels of the marshlands. (For during those ancient times, the fens were yet to be drained). The sight of their approach must have struck terror into the hearts of the villagers, for the cruelty and appearance of the invaders matched the mood of the cold sea from where they came.

It's a lonely spot and shrouded in myths and legends, I know, I've read about them in all these antique books I've acquired; I've quite a collection on my bookshelves here in the cottage. Relics and artefacts have been found in these fields dating to long before the Saxons … to the dawn of human history. Yes indeed … 'as old as time itself'.

Arthur Steens was the last owner and farmer of the land, but he died twenty years ago. He would have been the ogre who'd chased Milligan and I with his stick. According to the report in the regional paper, they fished his body from a pond. He had slipped and drowned in a drunken stupor, but the corpse had lain there for ages - a grisly spectacle. "Many an aquatic creature had obtained sustenance from the poor unfortunate's cadaver", so said the report, but there was no mention of the older man, his 'Da'. The Steens and their long-suffering wives had produced offspring with every generation, each one as bad as the other, but he was the last.

There were also several narratives of sheep and livestock going missing from the top field, or being found with their throats cut and drained of blood.

I passed further through the annals, reading articles and papers written by local historians and archaeologists. One provided a list of stories told by travellers over the passing centuries. I read a manuscript written by an abbot who had visited the village church of All Saints in the seventeenth century:

"Upon taking an evening's walk and contemplation upon a ridge with a view, I came across a ruin, and was confronted by a ghoul with eyes and a nose like that of a demon from Hell. The ogre did challenge me and threatened to drink my blood, but I held firm, and with great fortitude I recited The Lord's Prayer, and thus the

ghoul did recoil and scurry into the trunk of a tree – an ugly, gnarled sentinel, which I had not noticed before."

That struck a chord. There were accounts of witchcraft and so on – too many to mention – but there was also a copy of a translated text written by an early Christian monk. It was discovered in the crypt of the Saxon church and kept for posterity when the Normans rebuilt it, and renamed it 'All Saints'. It described how the village menfolk watched in horror when three Viking longboats crossed the waterways and marshlands lying to the east of the settlement:

"We counted our blessings at our foresight in employing masons to build a tower of stone to act as a lookout, so that we had time for our women and children to flee. But as the barbarians came upon us, our fortitude weakened, and the brutes began to hack us down. We would all have surely perished, had it not been for the occurrence of a ghoulish miracle. Quite suddenly, the bearded slayers dropped their swords and shields, froze, sank to their knees and lay stiff and prostrate. Savage war cries had waned to muted grunts, by clutching, clawing fingers upon throats. Their startled surprise turned to terror – a picture of Hell emblazoned within widened, glazed eyes – as blood poured through gripping fingers. Then, some invisible and unholy force dragged their feeble, struggling bodies towards the aged and bloated tree stump at the top of the rise. Its protruding roots seemed to suck them beneath the ground. We watched in awe, but we were indeed saved."

I sourced a more factual account from a book of local archaeology. It described the strange carvings on the stones they'd unearthed when they drained the fens during the eighteenth century. Viking runes for sure; they were preserved by the parish squire, and are now housed in the county museum. Of course, they couldn't be sure of the exact meaning, but it roughly translated as: *"Our warriors being devoured by a demon of wood brought to life."*

That same book went on to describe how the tower had been constructed on an earthen mound dating as far back as the Neolithic, and that sacred offerings and gifts were often found buried there.

I told Tom all this in the pub after another fruitless day at the office; another nail in the coffin of our failing business. "I have to return to the ridge," I said, "find out what made me feel so drained … so anxious. What about Anna? What if she's in danger?"

He looked at me in an odd way, as if to say: "The strain's getting to you old boy; you're retreating into realms of fantasy and avoiding reality. And it's *Anna*, now is it …?"

My phone rang at that moment.

"Ms. Esquivel; hello, I—"

How odd; how serendipitous.

But she'd interrupted me, and her voice had altered. She seemed less self-assured … anxious. "I really would like it if you could come right away to the barn … it is quite urgent that you do so."

Tom raised an eyebrow. He was reading me as you would an open book. "I'll wait for you in the pub then … lucky bastard."

***

I could not contain my excitement as I hurried along the pathway beside the church, and I arrived at the barn in half the time it had taken on my previous visit, albeit hot and breathless – it was still a sultry evening and the booze was affecting me.

My elation reverted to that familiar feeling of depression and despair when the eerie silence of my surroundings regained control. Just what was I getting into? I knew by the way her tone had changed that something was wrong.

Fools rush in ....

I re-entered the derelict building with trepidation. The door was stiff and unyielding, and the grinding noise of the hinges echoed around the empty chamber as I entered a realm of brooding shadows.

I called her name and waited for the female form to emerge from those shadows in dreadful anticipation; strange as I felt so deflated when she failed to appear.

I called again, but it was obvious I was alone.

It occurred to me that she may have taken a walk to the top field and to the folly and she had stumbled upon that queer old tree. Perhaps, her interest at my inane remark concerning the landscape's aesthetic merits wasn't feigned or patronising after all. At least that's what I hoped.

I set off in that direction, rushing and stumbling; the stuffy heat making me wheeze and sweat. But there was no-one to greet me; not a living soul. She was playing games with me. I cursed my foolishness;

she obviously 'got off' by teasing lonely, vulnerable men such as me.

… And yet, I wanted more.

I chose not to approach the folly because that dreadful sense of anticipation was getting to me. Instead, I skirted the top field below the crest in search of a decent shot for my camera. I always take it with me, wherever I ramble – you never know what visual delights the setting sun may proffer. Besides, a good one might impress Anna.

You see, I was trying to calm myself a bit, and … the further away the top field became, the less foreboding it was. I could think logically. The scene in front of me looked wonderfully Gothic and atmospheric – a dark and imposing keep on a ridge next to a blackened outline of a gnarled and decrepit tree.

The angry red of the sky was poking through an opening halfway up the tower; I hadn't noticed that before. It probably once formed a window; now it resembled a watching eye. I reeled off a few movie shots and stills, but got spooked. I decided I'd had enough, so I took the short-cut across the thistles and headed towards the school.

Forget her. Forget her.

By the time I'd returned to the cottage, my mood had lifted.

Before supper, I was eager to see what I had caught on camera, and so set about downloading the images on to the computer. The results were dramatic and Gothic, just as I had hoped – silhouettes of the tower and tree stark against the backdrop of a blood-red sunset. I congratulated myself.

Until I spotted it. Everything changed after that.

From that window of the tower – that *portal* – I saw it watching me; a figure, a *face* .... Something had been skulking around up there without my knowing. A finger traced its icy tip along my spine.

An apparition.

I tried all sorts of ways to magnify and enhance the image; what I was left with made me shudder. It was grainy, but a face, I was certain, and framed, no *trapped,* inside the portal ... with minute holes for eyes, and with her dishevelled, flowing hair black in the fiery glow of the sky .... And a whitened skull, with hollow eye-sockets, and grinning teeth. I was literally, staring at death in the face. I almost fell from my chair.

I began to play back the video footage – I had to. My mouth was dry as the monitor flickered. The figure remained, but amidst the awful, silent playback, it winked out. A patch of pale, translucent mist coalesced at the base of the tower. It was alive! It drifted purposefully towards the bole of that ugly tree. I paused the film and tried to magnify the image; I wanted to know what I was looking at, but it was very difficult given the poor resolution and lack of light.

A body, slender and graceful. A *body* ... with limbs spread, and gliding through the air in the twilight. But how? There had been no breeze and the air was still.

Definitely alive, leastways, not dead.

Slowly, slowly it drifted, drawn by the tree. I zoomed in on the apparition cowering between the gaps of the aged, rotten boughs - a head with a mane of long flowing hair and turned towards me.

That was enough; I pressed the scanner switch and extinguished the phantom. Recoiling, I staggered to the kitchen; I needed a glass of water.

I halted when I saw the display screen on my phone flicker; an incoming message. I barely recognised her voice, the way it wavered and sobbed, that is, until she spoke her name.

"Please, please, it's Anna … you must come … come now … help … *help me* …"

Then it went dead.

I played the message again, several times. She was pleading with me, her pitch so desperate. No longer aloof, no longer confident; it was such a shock.

I had to go back, and I had to go right away.

She was no tease, I knew that now. There was something malignant, something *evil* on that ridge, the nature of which horrified me, but even so, I felt compelled to go up there; she was in peril. Perhaps though, if I had allowed myself space to think matters through, I would have thought better of it.

The light was rapidly fading and I could just discern the tower and tree on the greying skyline. The sound of my laboured breaths continued to torment me in the humid air … and those of another: that small dog, panting and whining as it danced around my feet. I stooped, determined catch sight of it … to feel the warmth of its fur. There it was, white and pale in the gloom. It wanted to be my companion, to be at my side, but something wasn't quite right; its eyes were missing - empty, black pits and with a gaping jaw - and its skin was taut and dry across its bones as if it were decomposing.

Then it all kicked off.

The mutt was but one of many such animals. There were hundreds of them spilling from the crest and beyond - sheep, cattle, pigs, goats, wild pigs and aurochs from a bygone era, and other forest beasts I was unable to recognise; their bellows and baying echoing in the ether. Just like the dog, they were emaciated and, well ... *dead.* Long extinct beasts - wizened, dried cadavers, puffing dusty breaths - and others that were fresher and recently slaughtered, with carcasses covered in open, bloody wounds and sores as though savaged by a wild, unholy creature. Unearthly animated shapes milling in the twilight.

Suddenly a holler from over the animal din; it came from near the peak of the slope.

"Oi, kid, you're back! Come up here, c'mon. Did you bring yer football?"

Milligan!

This couldn't be. He was still the familiar urchin; school tie at half-mast, with grimy knees poking out from below his short trousers, and looking at me in that expectant manner. As he ran towards me, I caught the blooded scratches and sores on his skin - the same as those on the beasts.

I was unable to comprehend, it all happened so

quickly. I reeled at the cacophony of bloodcurdling shouts from the phantoms spewing over the ridge – hundreds of warriors – their barbaric cries resounding in my ears as they swarmed down the slope. I froze and cowered, until I realised they were ignoring me. They skirted around the circumference of the field, shouting and wailing, locked in combat. I recognised them; they were the Viking hordes I'd read about. A few strayed and drew close; I dared to look. Ghouls of the dead again, with skin dry and taut, stretched on blackened, grinning skulls. I recoiled in horror.

Another swarm emerged from the summit, but the garb was different; they were paler and translucent; swirling, luminant pools of mist, and their skulls were bleached white instead, and shone bright against the black. With what was left of my sense of reason, I supposed they were souls from a far earlier epoch. Maybe they were Neolithic people. I staggered aimlessly, gawping at the macabre spectacle.

The gates of time were opening, and displaying scenes of horror from the distant past.

Yet another wave, droves of them, with outlines and shapes less defined, and not human, judging by their stooping gait. And then I cottoned on by the protrusion of bone on their foreheads and stocky build that these were Neanderthals. This place was indeed *as old as time itself*.

The more ancient the spectres were, the more opaque and blurred the 'playback' – if that is what it was.

I had to get away.

I don't know how I found my resolve but I arose and stumbled towards the top amid the myriads of spectres wailing around me. I could see now that they were all emerging from that decrepit, squat shaped tree, which, I was certain, had taken the guise of the old man with the hooked nose. He beckoned me with his wiry, gnarled finger. This danse macabre was a roll call of souls that had fallen victim to whatever emanated from that hideous bole of the tree. A demon, whatever guise it took – a tree, an old man – it chopped, it butchered, it ate, it devoured.

I was but a few feet from the trunk, when I halted dead in my tracks. I gawped, dumbfounded. Whether everything vanished and reverted to nature, I cannot say, because I was only aware of what was in front of me:

Anna.

Too late.

Her body, pressed up against the trunk, was battered and bloodied, and her limbs were splayed and bound to its crust. Her hair, once so lush and vibrant, seemed welded onto the sticky blood stained bark.

She was the freshest and most recent victim, you see, but already her wrists and ankles began to dissolve as the wood creature started to absorb her, and so provide the relish for the ghoul's summer feast.

I fell to my knees and she stared down at me

with those large brown eyes, wide and filled with anguish. She wasn't so cool and self-assured now.

And she uttered a single word – "help."

Nothing more.

As she sank into the bark, I noticed most of her clothes were torn away … revealing her naked figure, a well-defined figure … *a figure which you would die for …*

But not me.

And once again, panic-stricken, *I ran … I ran like bloody hell.*

Woodchester Park, The Cotswolds

Afterwards

I have, as you know, always held a firm opinion that the concept of ghosts, the afterlife or anything of that kind was a product of the human imagination, taking the view that there are a myriad of other causes that would explain the witnessing of such phenomena, the most likely on each occasion providing a satisfactory conclusion. That said, if one *were* to encounter a preternatural event, it would probably go unnoticed. Imagine, if you will, a busy shopping mall; a sea of faces approaching you. The sun catches one of them – a figure misaligned, out of proportion, not belonging, but with its visage turned towards you with a fixed stare. A ghost? Or merely a trick of the light? No clanking chains or footsteps on creaking stairs, no wails of despair carried by the breeze on a stormy or moonlit night; such flights of fancy are the province of the story teller, by the fire on a cold, winter's evening.

That was my assertion until my reunion with my old friend Chad Saxton a few days ago. It has, I confess, left me shaken, and forced me to reassess my beliefs. It is an altogether humbling affair, but perhaps, without my knowing, it may have provided a denouement to the mystery of Greymere Woods that was already playing on my mind and quietly undoing my hitherto steadfast beliefs.

I first visited Greymere Woods ten years ago, the summer of '39 in fact. I remember it well; all that excitement regarding the excavations at Sutton Hoo – the archaeology, the unearthing of a Viking longship burial, with its priceless history and treasure …. Days of summer, optimism and discovery, and making hay while the sun shines; the lull before the storm and the call of arms, Hitler and war. Then, history, life, *everything*, was put on hold.

I began my army training near Gloucester, and, during a few days leave, had taken a hike to nearby Greymere. My mood was nonchalant and fatalistic at the thought of the coming conflict; I certainly wasn't troubled, at least on the surface, so there is no logical explanation as to why I found the place so strange, so spooky … so *depressing*. Try as I may, I could not put my finger on why. The woods consisted mainly of pine and I discovered a series of trails that circled the perimeter and descended into its interior, the basin of which formed a lake – a placid pool reflecting grey by the sky. Upon its surface, there was barely a ripple.

Trees of Scots pine, firs and spruce bore down from the steep banks hemming the tracks, and everywhere was so silent. There were no sounds of life – human or beast – no birds chattering in the boughs, nor the rustling of leaves, and everywhere was still and dormant in the cool, dank air. The verdant was tainted with a dull, washed-out patina, since the sun scarcely penetrated the canopy above; hence, the stillness, and the quietude of this seemingly perpetual, inert, shadowy domain. Up high, I could see the loftiest most boughs sway in a noiseless, distant breeze, like the teasing boa feathers of exotic dancers - a tantalising glimpse of the outside world.

Woods of conifer are, of course, deserts; devoid of the natural habitat of our fair and blessed land, the realm I loved and was about to defend.

Maybe it was because I was weary, or anxious as to my imminent posting abroad, but *something* made me feel uneasy. I can't even say that it was a primeval fear that a predator - human, beast or demon - was stalking me, it wasn't that, it just gave me the creeps. Perhaps I was picking up on negative vibes, that is, echoes of the past occurring in the landscape, but such notions didn't occur to me at the time. I mention that because I later discovered that the ridge and basin once formed an Iron Age hillfort and so was, no doubt, the pitch of many a bloody battle. Yes, negative vibes; I took it as a portent for what was to come. I'm told it overlooks the Severn Valley to the west, with views stretching as far as the estuary, and that there are ancient burial mounds scattered along the escarpment. It's hard to see; they're all obscured now by the trees, and therefore difficult to envisage.

Ah, those trees - the silent, watching sentinels.

Down one twisting, narrow path, lies a house constructed from Cotswold sandstone and built in Georgian, classical style, but it remains unfinished and has never been occupied. I recall the way it gleamed even in that overcast, sullen light, and how it appeared so pristine, almost sentient, if you'll permit my indulgence. As you approach you are presented with a portico entrance of Palladian columns, and under the eaves at each corner, there are gargoyles – ugly, gurning faces that look half monk, half devil – from whose dribbling mouths spat rainwater. I remember peering inside through the dusty sash windows, and spying the hallway with its lavish marble floor and opulent Doric columns that support the lofty roof of oak beams and stone lintels and corbels. They converged at the centre to a sunroof that captured no sun. Stairways surrounded the rectangular hall, and, I surmised, led to empty, unfinished rooms with offshoots of passages and unfulfilled destinations. It is, as I've explained, incomplete. The architect and owner remain a mystery to me, but there are hints of eccentricity and, dare I say, madness concerning the whole affair.

I thought it best to leave. Shadows were lengthening and a sixth sense was telling me to depart before nightfall – silly, I know. I ended up enquiring about the place at the local hostelry, trying not to appear too feeble of mind. The drinkers nodded, narrowed their eyes, glanced at each other, and presented a sly, collective smile. "Yes, it is supposed to be haunted …"

But by whom? Or what?

It is only now, after my meeting with Saxton, that I dwell on one particular cryptic comment made by the landlord, which at the time I dismissed of no importance. It went something along the lines of: "The woodland itself is waiting for a haunting –

manifesting into the form of an entity or phantom that an unsuspecting visitor unwittingly bestows upon it, and assuming its role or persona. Either way, you won't know until afterwards."

What on earth was he talking about?

But, there was a war to win, and I considered such self-indulgent posturings as melancholic and of no consequence.

A decade has since past and the matter was forgotten ... until a few days ago. Out of the blue, I received correspondence from Chad Saxton, the ex-army chum I mentioned, with whom I had trained at the camp. From there we had been posted to Egypt, but soon after we'd gone our separate ways. He was, I recall, a confident, outgoing fellow, and athletic too - always in rude health, with red cheeks, and a beaming smile - and had a restless manner about him. And, being of Saxon descent, not Prussian, had a particular yen for beating the Nazis. He joined The Secret Intelligence Service - MI6 or SIS - and was assigned secret duties, so we lost touch.

Saxton's unexpected letter was fairly innocuous. He wrote that he was back in Blighty, fancied a nostalgic tour and intended to visit the old training barracks and surrounding area and did I want to come along for the recce?

We met at the very same inn I visited on the day I got spooked out at Greymere Woods. He was sitting in an alcove in the snug, behind the fireplace, where only the glow from the burning logs in the hearth penetrated. The first thing that struck me was his manner and appearance. He'd lost weight, looked gaunt, and, although it was difficult to tell in the dimness, I'd swear he was unshaven. He had aged for sure, and I was drawn to his downturned mouth and sunken eyes – The War had taken its toll.

Conversation was a little stilted; he'd 'seen things' was his evasive answer when I enquired as to his service in special ops, and, although he was willing to pay his share for drinks – whisky, several of them – he insisted that I go to the bar and fetch them. I duly obliged and on one occasion enquired with the landlord how long he'd been there waiting for me.

He cocked his head quizzically, peered at the corner of the snug hidden behind an oak beam and drew a blank look. He said nothing, but smiled knowingly as if he'd suddenly cottoned on to who I was. I guess by the glint in his eye that he'd recollected me from when I first enquired about Greymere, in spite of the intervening years.

I returned to the snug with the drinks, fronting a cheery disposition, determined to rekindle our comradeship and make a day of it. I related my encounter in Greymere Woods – it seemed an obvious opener for discourse – in the hope it would galvanise him. "It lies no more than half a mile from the village, across the main road, and overlooks the escarpment."

He raised his head unexpectedly, the light from the bar catching his eyes, and they sparked with life – the first time they had.

"Ghosts? Hauntings? We should investigate. I've seen things. The site is abandoned you say, never occupied? I have sleeping bags. We should explore and have a sleepover in the hall. I can break in; easy by my standards. What say you, old chap?"

This was more like it - more of what I expected of him. I accepted with verve.

We set off, buoyed with whisky, oblivious of the dying light of the late winter afternoon. We walked the trail – the spiralling dirt tracks amid the firs – down, down, towards the brooding mere and the dimming, grey-green shades encompassing us. Bats flitted and swooped from the boughs to the mirror surface of the lake. "They're feasting on the moths and mayflies," I said rather pointlessly. It was of no interest to him.

The passing ten years meant nothing - the stillness, the quietude, the *inertness*, and the lack of sentient life, all prevailed. It hemmed us in and was stifling. We must have spent a couple of hours trudging, but there was still no resolution as to the mystery of Greymere Woods.

Saxton hardly spoke a word during our descent into the depression that led to the house, merely grunting at my inane comments as to why I found the location so creepy. Rain clouds were forming - more brooding than thunderous - and it was getting dark. The trees were blurring, merging into featureless, ghostly shapes.

"We'll get wet if we are unable to gain entry to the house." My voice sounded hollow in the sombre air.

He didn't answer; instead he stole me a glance,

and withdrew a crowbar and pliers from his knapsack. The chain and padlock imprisoning the hallway yielded with surprising ease, and he had pushed aside the heavy oak doors underneath the portico with indifference, indicating that such an act did not merit discussion. We took a few hesitant steps inside, craning our necks this way and that, awed by the opulence of the lofty chamber. Our boots echoed on the pearly white marble floor, which gleamed as bright as the sandstone walls outside, in spite of the pervading dullness. But a sudden gust through the open door – an unnatural breeze, I thought – soiled the pure white with detritus from the forest floor. It told us – *told me* – that we weren't supposed to be there.

I wanted to understand more than ever what haunted the place; my frustration as potent as my angst.

"We should make camp," Saxton declared.

Military life had not left him. He unloaded his knapsack, unfurled the sleeping bags – they appeared to be army surplus – and lit the portable gas camping stove. It was if he were on manoeuvres, or a mission; there was no eye contact and his manner was impassive. I feared that he considered the whole affair a bit of a disappointment, but when I suggested that to him he harrumphed, and his mood altered. He seemed to want to explain something to me but didn't know how, and so had given up.

But then, over a hearty meal of bacon, eggs, coffee, chocolate and whisky, he began to open up.

We talked about this and that – our army training days, good ale, fishing, chess, comrades and what happened to them and had he kept in touch with them after The War (to which he shook his head); and women … or rather the lack of them in our lives.

Whatever; I'd resigned myself to not having shown him, or indeed myself, that ghosts existed. I said as much to him.

"You think?" was his retort. He strode to the nearest window and threw open the boards. "Come …"

A wall of blackness confronted me; night had fallen. I watched. I listened. The breeze had picked up and threw pulses of rain at the boards and windowpanes – pitter-patter in rhythmic tattoos. I craned my neck to a bright, starry firmament in search of the offending clouds, their presence betrayed by the constellations winking out and relighting. Weird voices wailed and fluted in the eaves above us; a gathering of uneasy spirits; a visitation from the dense curtain of pines as they muttered and whispered in the murk. The woods were alive after all.

But an illusion fired by imagination. No ghosts.

Saxton listened too. I could tell by his raised chin, but he never spoke, and his expression was robbed from me by the dark. The pause was interminable, until he sighed and returned to his berth. I secured the window board and followed suit. I extinguished the burner, more afraid of what the light-glow would reveal than that of the dark itself.

Then, he related the strangest of tales ….

"It was January 1945, the dying months of The War, and I was working undercover for the SIS, and posing as a German infantryman from what was left of the retreating Wehrmacht as they fled from the onslaught of the Red Army swarming through East Prussia towards its capital, Koenigsberg. My mission was to assess the exact strength and numbers of the Soviets, and how far they would advance along the Baltic coast, past Danzig, towards Jutland and Admiral Doenitz's operations centre at Flensberg, before they linked up with the British and Canadians. The boys in Whitehall were thinking ahead – just how much resistance the Germans were prepared to put up would determine the extent of the Russians' advance in the West. Our American friends seemed indifferent at that time to our concerns.

"Anyway, I got involved, and embroiled. I thought I wouldn't but I overestimated my resolve. I became sweet on a woman; Hilde, her name was, a widow. Her husband had copped it at Stalingrad and she was left with an infant daughter. I'd met her in a village five miles from Koenigsberg when I assumed my alias identity and had blended in with the ragtag survivors of the many units, civilians and stragglers who were preparing the defences of the city's perimeter. She was in a bread queue, infant clutching at her arm, when a skirmish broke out and she fell to the ground. I heard her screaming, searching frantically for her child, then the bombs rained down. I pushed through the melee, grappled bread from a surly thug – I recognised him as a junior SS officer, disguised in civvies in an attempt to escape his crimes – gave her the bread and rescued the child. I'll never forget her tears of gratitude.

"Koenigsberg fell – of course it did. The wagons of refugees rolled on through the sloping forests, heading for the port of Gotenhafen in the hope of boarding a ship that would cross the Baltic and deliver them to northern Germany or the east coast of occupied Denmark. With all but a modicum of my mission's aim remaining, I joined the wagon train. There was still hope, and, I admit, camaraderie within our company of stricken souls that we would prevail, and, to my joy, Hilde and the infant were among us!

"That wily fellow, Grand Admiral Doenitz, U-boat chief and scourge of our merchant navy, was organising a mass evacuation by a flotilla of ships. He'd mustered what vessels that were still seaworthy and could lay his hands on – obsolete destroyers, pre-war cruise ships, even fishing boats. It was reminiscent of Dunkirk, but on a grander scale. We were hoping to board the The Wilhelm Gustloff, an ageing transport ship, but it meant traversing a forest, a forest not unlike this …"

He broke off his account, and raised the flame on the burner. Its flare washed his sunken cheeks a pallid yellow, and his haunted eyes searched the surrounds of the hall like flitting fireflies. "A pine forest of slopes, hollows and depressions with cold, brooding lakes, silent in the blanketing snow, save for the baying of hungry wolves lurking in the moonlight shadows ….

"The wagons were sitting ducks. We were strafed by Stukas. People were screaming and dying. Leastways, we got separated and, amid the chaos, scattered into groups. There were five of us: me, Jurgen, Karl, Hilde and the child. We found shelter for the night at an abandoned woodcutter's hut. The men went searching, under cover of the dark, for food and a short-cut down to port. I stayed with Hilde; I had wounds that needed tending. Earlier, back in Koenigsberg, we had made love, she, I expect, with gratitude and stoicism – such was the price for my saving her from the brutalities of war – but now, here, as we warmed ourselves beside a fire of crackling splinter-wood, I hoped it was more from affection and love; that's what I like to think. She dressed my wounds, and sated my needs, both physical and otherwise; of that I'm certain …."

He paused, bit his lip and shook his head. "They must have seen the glow of the fire – The Reds – they came in droves, sudden and ferocious, from over the crest; I reckon they'd encamped somewhere behind the rows of larch. They bounded down the snowy slope – a pack of wolves, black against the moonlit snow – chasing our two compatriots just ahead of them. We had to make a decision, and fast. Jurgen, the fittest among us, stole away with the woman and child, while Karl and I would attempt to hold them off.

"And … this is the thing, this is the *thing* …" He pointed his finger at me, and his eyes flared. "When they were upon us, we could see they weren't human, no … their faces were those of *wolves* with angry, yellow, beady eyes, and out of their muzzles, canines protruded, from which saliva drooled. No skin, no flesh, but fur of grey, and yet, they were upright as men, and clad in khaki with boots and clutching rifles. Foul and visceral. I'd heard numerous legends and folklore of such beasts roving the outlands of north-eastern Europe that date back for generations: The Külming … wolf creatures with canines but with horns as well, hunting and marauding the Baltic forests. The Külming, yes … they're actually restless spirits of the unholy dead – in this case, fallen Russian soldiers."

His tired eyelids grew heavy and sank. He sighed and turned his back to me.

"Well, what happened? Chad, please tell me."

He buried himself in the sleeping bag. With an air of resignation, I was left to wonder what kind of hallucinations would have manifested in his brain, given the stress and trauma of the situation he'd endured, especially when compounded with tricks the light would bestow in a dark and numbing, snowbound winter forest.

But he hadn't done. "I got word that Hilde had successfully crossed the ice sheets of the Vistula Lagoon and reached Gotenhafen. I think she boarded the Wilhelm Gustloff; that's the one that was torpedoed by the Soviet submarine, S-13. It picked them off, and other vessels once they were out to sea. I can only speculate as to whether she was among its many victims. I can't bear the thought of her lying at the bottom of the cold waters of the Baltic, drowned and forgotten amid the horrors of war. Well … at any rate, I never saw my Hilde, the beautiful woman with the loving eyes, again."

I considered it both pointless and insensitive to pursue the conversation further. I listened to the bats roosting above us, as restless as my thoughts, then I must have fallen asleep.

We woke at first light. Saxton seemed anxious to get away. He packed his belongings with discourteous haste, and when he paused at the door and looked at me, his visage was as grey and ashen as the dawn. I saw something I hadn't noticed before – the clawlike scars across his sallow cheeks.

"Glad we met up, old chap," he said, "glad I got that off my chest, but I'll make my own way from here." With that he left.

After I had gathered my belongings, I searched the trail leading to the road, but he'd disappeared.

If you have read my narrative thus far, you will conclude that, upon my second visit to Greymere Woods, that no supernatural event occurred, and so you will be curious as to what therefore, has caused me to quell my conviction that no such phenomena exist.

I was determined to pursue my reacquaintance with Saxton. I got in touch with my old regiment's adjutant, Smith.

"Saxton?" he mused with a raised eyebrow. "You don't know? Well, I suppose you wouldn't. He was working undercover on the Eastern Front in the winter of '44 to'45, SIS, MI6 and all that. He bought it, somewhere out in the Rominten forest. We know that because the Russians found his security tag. Terrible wounds apparently – claw marks. Perhaps the wolves got him. Difficult to be certain, coming from these Russky fellows. Awful shame though."

I thought about my opening premiss that it is reasonable to suppose that one may be unaware as to whether they have ever encountered a ghost, and then I remembered the landlord's remark after my first experience in Greymere Woods:

" ...The woods ... waiting for a haunting ... an unsuspecting visitor bestows upon it ... either way, you won't know until afterwards."

A friend once challenged me to write a ghost story about a lighthouse keeper and how the isolation and solitude would encroach upon him; instead I came up with this. Not quite what he had in mind, but the same underlying theme.

A foray into science fiction, but a true ghost story nonetheless.

Terminus

"Gramps used to call me a child of the moon,"Nereid says to me during repose – the moment before we enter the next period of sleep-time.

It's a tale she's told me many times, and always when she emerges from the shadows in the rest-sphere, just as the pin-sharp lights above me extinguish in the low ceiling, and the entire station is bathed in the aquamarine hues of the Neptunian atmosphere far below us. The calming iridescence soothes me as it seeps through the porthole, crosses the floor and creeps over my bed.

I welcome her; it's my favourite bedtime story, and it helps me to forget that we are the last souls remaining on this lonely frontier: Terminus – end of the line, the outermost staging post of the Solar System and orbiting Neptune. None of the ion-drive freighters and liners go beyond this point. From here on, only the new high-energy plasma fuelled rockets venture further into the black and icy depths of the Kuiper Belt, where the Sun shines no stronger than a bright yellow star in the heavens; a twinkling speck illuminating the myriad tiny worlds of ice hiding out there. They watch me like ghosts in the dark.

She stands before me in a white nightgown with naked calves and feet, pallid and cold; her face obscured by the blue light. It masks her thoughts; secrets untold. She seems unsure whether she should approach me but begins her story anyway:

"My father was the last miner on Mars to leave. The Conglomerate had deemed the entire terraforming project a failure and declared it as officially cancelled. It was the dust storms, you see; the technology was available, but the investors were no longer prepared to stump up the money. Life was tough, even for hardened veterans such as my father. Starved of resources, his comrades had returned home the previous Martian summer while they could and before the climate grew too harsh. All were ill or dying; their will broken. They were penniless too of course; the Corporation had, they insisted, broken their contracts. Bastards.

"My father was certain they could have made the whole thing work, given time, but how could they fill the dry ocean beds and rift valleys from the vast subterranean reservoirs before they'd equalised the atmospheric pressure? Too much haste born from government impatience and corporate greed.

"His final task was to decommission the last of the working pit shafts on the surface – the one based near the foothills of the Elysium Tholi mountains. It wouldn't do for a rival conglomerate to acquire any abandoned infrastructure.

"The dust-strewn plains of the north were where most of the mining occurred, especially in the Elysium quadrant. All of those extinct volcanoes – portals to the underworld and the subterranean labyrinth of caves deep below – led the miners to believe they'd found heaven and unimaginable riches down there. I suppose it was the name that drove and inspired them – Elysium, derived from the Elysian Fields – the Greek land of heaven and plenty and the place you go to in the afterlife. Don't you see?"

She pauses, waiting for my response, and I nod, noticing how intense her manner is.

"It was anything but during those final days, when failure hung over them. 'Harsh, cold and unforgiving', my father told me. The energy supply for the life support systems would barely sustain him before the last shuttle home, and food was on ration. He was, they said, allowed to salvage anything for himself and his own profit, provided it complied with certain regulations and weight restrictions, and, subject to him completing his assignment. That's why he worked like a dog – from dawn until dusk – avoiding the deadly chill of the Martian night … why he eked out the meagre supplies provided for him as best he could. Then he could begin to salvage anything they considered worthless for his own gain, and so get one up on the Conglomerate … but I think *that* was the beginning of the end for him.

"Everyday, just before daybreak, when it was still bitterly cold, and in spite of having the thermal settings on his spacesuit set to a bare minimum for as long as he could endure in order to conserve the failing batteries, he would trek across the surface – a whole kilometre – towards the foothills using the land-hopper. He'd watch the diminutive moon, Phobos, glide over the azure sky – the colour of the Martian dawn. It rose in the west and set in the east as if defying nature, and in the time it took him to make the journey; nothing more than a dark, irregular shaped boulder, just 3,700 miles above him, arcing silently and eerily beyond the rarefied atmosphere. As black as soot, it blotted out the twinkling stars as it headed towards the distant mountains on the horizon; a sinister patch of darkness that stained the vista of jewels above as though it were a salient, brooding entity. It seemed to follow him … watch him, and he could sense the evil.

"Sometimes, when exhaustion from his labours got the better of him, he would stop and stare up at its surface and imagine there were creatures writhing and wriggling in the shadows cast among its hills and crevices. Maybe it was a result of the slow oxygen starvation he had inflicted upon himself in order to defy the Corporation's greed … it brought on a bout of space sickness. He often used to say he felt an overwhelming desire to rip off his helmet and breathe the fragrant air that he convinced himself existed. An illusion … and an allegory akin to the Elysian Fields ….

"Each day as he trudged across the plain, the worm-like creatures grew more vivid, until eventually, limbs appeared on their bodies – two arms, two legs, and a head. They groped and clawed through the soot. He gazed with a mixture of fascination and horror, until Phobos sank once more below the horizon. But the nagging certainty of witnessing the same macabre display enact the next day and the next would gnaw at his mind. He'd swear the rocky moon drew closer to the surface each time.

"He fought against his fear, determined to see his task through to the end, otherwise the Corporation would have won, and he would be unable to retrieve any salvage; he'd be left with nothing.

"Then, on the final day, it broke him. On his outward journey to the rig, one of the creatures broke free from the squirming mass – a tiny speck floating in the sky. He studied the being from his binoculars – no worm – he saw her flowing hair, her limbs and her delicate hands glide and disappear somewhere behind the foothills.

"Do you know what 'Phobos' means?" Nereid asks me halfway through her narrative. "Phobia is the Roman god of fear, and fear ate away at my father during that last day at the rig. He would have started on the return trip well ahead of sunset had it not been for the loading of the auto-wagons with his precious salvage, and the million other tasks to complete before the pithead could be sealed forever.

"As it was, he was forced to repair to his dwelling in the twilight, and it was then that she came to him. She emerged from the foothills, flying and swooping towards him with an unnatural speed. He watched her as he drove, craning his neck anxiously in all directions, afraid of losing sight of her. She stood in front of the land-hopper, forcing him to stop and barring his way; her hair and robe billowing in a non-existent breeze. The air-lock opened with a hiss – the sound of her sigh – and he invited her in. Her face and skin were as white and iridescent as the permafrost on the foothills from where she appeared, and yet when the robe slipped from her flesh, his fear melted. She looked at him with eyes of translucent cobalt blue as her blackened lips pressed on his. Her embrace completed the union, and they made love that very night. He cried in her arms, lamenting his lot, but in the morning – the day of his departure from Mars – she was gone.

"He returned to Earth on one of the oldest ion-drive freighters that was still in service – it was all the Corporation was willing to provide – with me, a tiny bundle in his arms. You see, I was conceived and born by the she-being in a single night."

Nereid falls silent and studies me. It's hard to tell whether she believes in what she says, or is testing me. Her lips form a half-smile. "Well … that's the story Gramps told me; I *am* a child of the moon – Phobos, the moon.

"But as I grew and matured, I began to suspect otherwise. My father sank into vice – gambling and drink – and fell in with a crowd of thugs and crooks. I think my real mother was a whore he'd met in the drinking dens of Moon-base 14 en route back from Mars, the ultimate step of his passage home. He bought her services with the gold dust he'd salvaged at Elysium. A year later, he used more of the same to buy me from the whore and her pimp when he heard they wanted to use me for their clients' gratification, so I suppose he spared me from all of that. At least I reckon it was Moon-base 14, because that's where he eventually ended up with a knife in his back after a drunken brawl.

"Of course, I cannot prove any of this, any more than I can Gramp's 'child of the moon' tale. I don't know the whore's name or what she looked like, if she ever existed, but I think the alluring creature that descended from the rock of Phobos, is far more romantic a notion, don't you?

"Either way, my grandfather - Gramps - raised me. He brought me here to Terminus, still calling me his 'child of the moon' and only after my continued asking as to how long will I reside here, would he answer. He said I would have to wait for someone to take my place. He'd force a smile and joke, 'Oh, it could be as long as a hundred years', or he'd turn reticent and avoid my questioning him further on the matter."

"But what do you do here? And where would you go?" I'm fascinated by her now and watch her standing in the shadows by the window of the rest-sphere, the pale wash of her gown barely perceptible. She's pondering, deep in thought, then looks at me. Her eyes, once as black as beads, flash like blue crystal as the glow from the swirling clouds of Neptune catches them momentarily.

No answer.

I *want* to make love to her, but … she's half my age. I *think* she wants me too, but it feels wrong, and yet …

"I'm glad you're here to keep me company," I say instead and with a sigh.

"Gramps left with the station's crew on the last travel liner back to Earth. They're no longer needed and the station is due to be fully automated. He says I should stay and wait to greet the explorers when the plasma-drives arrive back from the outer wastes, and only then can I follow him. I didn't know you would be here."

"Just a one-man maintenance crew, that's me; all that's required. It's a long time before the expeditionaries will reappear - well over two years - and there is but a skeleton crew of pilots, navigators and geologists on-board each one. It reminds me of the early pioneering days - an intrepid field-trip through the Kuiper Belt, to Pluto, Eris and beyond."

Nevertheless, the thought of being stuck out here all alone on Terminus dwells on me. I didn't appreciate that when I applied for the job. However, it requires little aptitude or effort and the servo-robots take care of the more complex issues - that reassures me.

Besides, I don't much care for the company of humankind now, not since Miranda left me. And yet … with the passing of each sleep-time and wake-time,

I'm finding less and less to keep me occupied, so I'm grateful that Nereid is here.

She's still looking at me with those eyes, and her smile broadens – a knowing smile. I must have been thinking aloud.

I hear the swish of the automatic door and she's vanished into the gloom again. I am alone once more.

***

The red light from the monitor flashes intermittently then stops altogether. I try to forget about it as I undertake my chores throughout wake-time and my dreaming of Nereid in between, but it returns, over and over, like a persistent spider crawling from a plug-hole. It unsettles me; it's a creeping phobia. The crimson glow is threatening and starkly out of place amidst the soft sheens of artificial light during wake-time, and the blue vaporific hues of Neptune during sleep-time.

I have no choice but to investigate and trace the source of the fault; red, is after all, a portent of danger, but I'd much rather be doing other things, such as dreaming about Nereid. Where is she?

I run a few diagnostics and discover there's a fault at the far end of the gantry scaffold; the vast tower of girders that stretch a mile from the lowest level of Terminus into the haze of Neptune's churning storms in its upper atmosphere. It's a limitless ocean of plasma energy, which they harness as fuel for the Kuiper Belt explorer craft. The monitor indicates there is a contaminant but I don't know what that means. A foreign body? Something that shouldn't be there and is trying to get in?

At least there's no immediate danger, the source having been located at the station's extreme edge. I'm lucky it's not the docking bays and so it won't concern the returning explorers when they eventually arrive. Or life support … then I'd have a real problem on my hands.

I check for the availability of servo-mites – mobile automatons with measuring devices and repair tools – but I've no need to worry because I can see two of them already on their way as they automatically home in on the damaged area. I hear the faint hiss of the probe portals open and catch sight of the diminutive insect-like objects descend the gantry and blur into the deep blue haze. It's curious to observe these rounded six-legged 'beasts' crawling down the girders; they use their limb-like pistons and suction cups with surprising dexterity.

The red light flickers more rapidly, increasing my angst, but I can do nothing other than put my faith in the ability of the servo-mites, and so I go about my duties (keeping an anxious eye on the beating, tormenting bulb every other minute). I'd sooner it sound an alarm, rather than afflict me with its constant and silent flashing on and off, on and off ….

Everything else seems fine – life support and the recycling systems – so no need for any maintenance there for at least three wake-cycles. I prepare a meal, and settle down in front of the images I like to watch on my bedside monitor. It's funny how film from my past creates happy reminiscences, but which are for the most part, untrue. False memory syndrome, they call it; hopes and wishes conjured up from the heart and mind replacing actual events.

Miranda, her eyes and the way she smiled contentedly; a future settled. I *thought* we were happy. False memories …

I look at the movie father took of me in the virtual-museum. I was a child and I'm standing on one of the old railway stations they used as transport terminals back on Earth centuries ago - on the last station terminus at the end of the line in the dead of night, where the platform lights taper to a point in the distance. It stretches to infinity - into a void of darkness and the unknown.

It's the same feeling I get here on Terminus when I gaze from the viewing deck.

I think the red light has stopped. I hold my breath, daring to hope …yes, it has. Joy.

I wonder when it stopped? I got so absorbed with thoughts of Miranda, that I forgot to check.

I move over to the observation window with a spring in my step and wait for the returning servo-mites to re-emerge from the haze. There they are, one … two … three. They climb the gantry as though they were living, sentient beings, and I'd swear there is an air of triumphalism as they march.

I'm distracted by a fleeting shadow from the corridor, and expect to glimpse Nereid with her lingering smile, but she isn't there. No matter, it's fine. I expect she'll come to me just before sleep-time.

Wait a minute…

Three? I counted three of them. But only two of them emerged from the hold earlier, I'm certain of that.

I peer out of the window again, my thoughts racing, and fear encroaching on me. I notice two insect-like robots redocking. I must have imagined the third.

***

Sleep-time.

Nereid hasn't appeared and it's unsettled me a bit.

Maybe it's because of my obsessive maudlin over Miranda; Nereid's told me before that it's not good for me to dwell on the past, and then she's become distant – aloof, I suppose you could say. Her manner alters and causes me to feel insecure and I don't want that to happen again. Perhaps I should go look for her. I tried that once, but I got lost amid the myriad of staff quarters on the lower decks (now deserted, of course) so I gave up. She could have been anywhere, and besides, it wouldn't do to stalk her. I'm sure she'll come to me … when she's ready.

I lie awake, and then I realise why. The iridescence of Neptune's bathing colours in the rest-sphere, always so sleep inducing and calming, isn't right. It's tainted with red; it's scarcely perceptible, and yet it plays on my mind. Oh …

I sit bolt upright in my bed. The red light from

the small panel on the opposite wall is flashing again – the source of the poisonous, crimson hue.

I walk to the control room aft, taking rapid strides. Instinctively, I squint from the main observation deck, down along the gantry towards its distant, tapering point, invisible in the Neptunian atmosphere's rage.

There!

A movement. An object, rocking about, and struggling to maintain its grip on the gantry. Perhaps there *was* a third servo-mite, after all. Maybe it's still effecting repairs, or its suction cups and piston limbs have failed and locked. I can't see it properly, and when I try to focus my eyes on it, its features become lost in Neptune's glare.

"Don't worry. Calm yourself." I hear her voice from behind me. "It comes and goes. I've resided on Terminus a lot longer than you, remember. Waiting …"

Nereid stares at me from the shadows, and my heart skips a beat. She's forgiven me. All thoughts of Miranda forgotten.

The flashing red light has stopped and I've lost sight of the object crawling on the gantry. I turn to Nereid but she's already fading into the darkness of the corridor. I wish she'd retell the story about Gramps, her father and the she-being; I long to know how she came to be.

It comes and goes. Does she mean the flashing of the bulb … or the clinging object?

I revert my gaze to the viewing port and to the

empty firmament, but whichever way I look, from any window, up and down, the vastness that is Neptune dominates with its majestic hegemony; a homage to its deific namesake. The twisting eddies of hydrogen and helium vapour are azure and poisoned with methane. They are whipped into whirlpools and hurricanes of unimaginable ferocity, and glow every shade of cerulean with each flash of plasma lightning, and yet it is all so eerily silent in the vacuum of space. White clouds of ammonia compounds scud across this infinite ocean. The richness of blue and white mimic a new Earth – a deadly deception, but it reminds me of home.

The orb of Triton – a shining pearl that is Neptune's massive moon – rises above the horizon. It spews out its invisible hydrogen, igniting forks of plasma lightning in Neptune's magnetosphere, but the whole vista appears so serene. It makes the dull, blue speck in the lower quadrant – the real Earth – seem so insignificant, and I realise how far from home I am.

***

Many sleep and wake-times have passed, and I've grown accustomed to the warning light. I know what's coming: Every time it starts up again, the object appears on the gantry, edging closer towards Terminus, in spite of its struggles.

I don't think it's a rogue servo-mite, although it does have limbs, a head and a torso, I'm pretty sure. It seems to be wrapped in a fabric or similar material, because I notice it flapping in the swirling, cosmic wind generated from the chaos below, but as I say, when I attempt to look at it directly, its head – if that is what it is – blurs and bleaches into the dazzling eddies.

I can't tell whether it's concentrating on its climb … or me.

And then the red light stops, and it disappears.

In between my chores, I've searched the data banks for details concerning the miners and the abandoned settlements on Mars, but I haven't found a great deal. There's an account of one Gunson Daak, the last mining engineer to leave Mars, who caused a great deal of disquiet on his journey home on the final transporter to desert the frontier towns in the north quadrant. In between bouts of aggression and hysteria, he mentioned a creature that emerged 'from the boulder in the sky' (Phobos) who had come to get him. Oxygen deficiencies combined with overwork were the cause of such hallucinations, it was concluded. Apparently he met a violent death somewhere among the drinking dens that pervade the seedier quarters of the obsolete Lunar transport terminals.

It certainly ties in with Nereid's story but – here's the thing – all this happened nearly a century ago. I wonder if she's picked this narrative up from the databank too.

But why would she invent such a tale? And for what purpose?

It's put me slightly on edge about her.

Nevertheless, I'd hate for her to find me checking up on her like this; I might lose her trust.

I seem to be getting on edge about a lot of things just lately. The creature – I call it that – has progressed further up the gantry now. I can see its white robe and dark hair waving around in the silent wind, with its body illuminated on the structure by the reflective opalescence of Triton. But when I look straight at it, its visage eludes me. It unnerves me how I can only watch it from beyond my peripheral vision, with my face to one side; it adds to my angst.

Perhaps it is me who's suffering from an onset of space sickness. I once heard talk of the possibility of ethereal beings existing inside the gas clouds of Saturn. It's an intriguing ghost story told by the early pioneers of the Solar System, but could it actually be true? Could the same thing be happening out here on Neptune?

And still, the red light pulses when the climbing creature appears.

Sleep-time begins and Nereid comes …

"I know you told me not to worry, but the warning light … I suppose I ought to do something about it."

"Next wake-time," she says and in the blue twilight the malignant pulses beat faster and cast a wash of scarlet across her pale skin. Her smile turns crooked and morphs her expression; there is predation in her eyes.

***

The older versions of the servo-mites are large enough to accommodate an operator. They are identical in all other aspects to the newer ones in that they are able to perform diagnostics and automatically repair any damage or malfunctions on Terminus, but have the added advantage of a human pilot. Most have been replaced by the more expendable and less risky automated servo-mites, but stations such as Terminus have always retained one of these outmoded type of craft in reserve.

I must admit that I've been dreading this moment and putting it off, but I've just realised whilst getting kitted out, and checking the instruments and so forth that it's helped to focus my mind. I can view things more rationally.

I've briefed Nereid on the operations of the air-lock controls, and, with a curl of her lip and a slight nod, I'm fairly confident that she'll perform her task well.

If it's a piece of space debris that's flapping about down there, or a sheet of metal plating that's torn free from either the gantry or one of the servo-mites, it must be removed, and either retrieved or cast adrift, otherwise the effectiveness of the sensory instruments might be impaired. Worse – if it collides and ruptures the intake structure for collecting and storing the plasma energy from the atmosphere then ….

Best not to dwell on that.

If only I could see the object clearly. It's definitely closer. It's baffling me.

I think the temporary respite from my fear is over. No wonder these archaic repair modules were decommissioned; I'm encased in a tube of metal with a transparent bubblelike dome inches from my head, and the spider legs of the craft are picking their way precariously down the girders of the gantry, wobbling and hesitating as though they were going to lose their grip at any moment and send me hurtling into the whirlpooling storm-clouds below.

Above me, the space-station shrinks from view, and all around me the purple winds rage and rattle against the dome, buffeting against the craft and causing it to sway. The aged and creaking hydraulics of the legs stall and the hull vibrates noisily, and I can actually hear the storm's rage, fizzing and crackling, and rising in pitch. As I gaze transfixed into the maw of the spinning hurricane, the clouds part and reveal the being – the creature – still edging along the girders towards me.

She's clear and iridescent with the winds billowing her gown, and exposing the pale flesh of her calves and feet. Her dark hair flaps – no, it *undulates* – around her. It reaches to her waist. I wish she would look directly at me so that I could see her face.

A dwarfish moon breaches the vast horizon of Neptune; the rocky boulder-shaped world they call Nereid, her namesake. Nereid: a sea nymph, bare-footed and dressed in white silk robes, and in attendance to the god Neptune. I'd forgotten that. How could I have done?

A child of the moon.

She's upon me now and she presses the palms of her hands upon the glass canopy enclosing me. She looks directly into my soul, and I feel her arm reach through the glass and press at my heart with an icy grip.

I understand now.

As the servo-mite reverses, and with her arms at the controls, she leaves me behind, but I see her head turn and look at me for the last time. I catch the stare of her jet-black eyes for a heartbeat before her face blurs once more.

I drift further down the tower of metal into the maelstrom and the deafening roar, my mind floating free from my body.

She would, I expect, explain to the explorers when they return many years hence, that I'd cast myself adrift, having gone mad from solitude and space sickness.

As for me, I'll stay here, all alone, in the outer reaches, clinging on to the edge of a precipice for ever and ever. Or, at least until some time in the distant future, a hundred years, perhaps, when I can lure someone down here and take my place.

Then, I'll begin my climb.

Michelham Priory, East Sussex
Dedicated to the grieving.

The Rowan Tree

"It's here where she appears ... on the landing. First by the display case beside me, then she glides down the corridor, her gown shining in the early glimmer of dawn, and yet curiously still – it doesn't waver in the air. I see patches of light passing for footsteps flitting along the polished floorboards … and its over in a matter of seconds; she disappears through the wall and flits across the gardens."

"Hmm …" Eckersley stared out of the oriel window at the far end of the hallway as he listened to my account, his back turned to me, hands clasped behind him. "I notice the road beyond the gatehouse is visible from here even on a dark winter's day such as this, in spite of the distance."

"What of it?"

"Hmm …" He turned round and walked towards me, his hand brushing the rail crowning the summit of the vast oak staircase that lay opposite the display cabinets. This was the centrepiece of the manor's grand restoration. "Does the road carry a lot of early morning commuter traffic?"

"Yes, I suppose."

"Hmm …" He pursed his lips this time, raised his eyebrow and glanced behind me; something had caught his attention. "I see you've kept her dress, the white one, her favourite; it's hanging on the door of the wardrobe." He threw me an awful look; a cross between pity and admonishment. He may as well have said, "that is unhealthy."

"I've told you before, that has nothing to do with it."

"It may have everything to do with it; you're still grieving. How long is it now?"

"It'll be a year this December. Anyway, I expected you to be installing an array of gadgetry by now, you know – infra-red cameras, instruments for measuring psychic activity, trip wires, scattering powder in order to detect footprints; a whole plethora."

"'Fraid not, old boy; have to be objective, even though we're best buddies; the Society for Psychical Research would not approve and I've been appointed vice-president, so I've a reputation to maintain. No, all that comes if, and only if, we decide on further investigation. However …"

He pulled a compass from his breast pocket. "Dawn, you say? The oriel faces due east …."

He retraced his steps on the landing and they echoed around the stone walls. "I'd like to take a stroll to the gatehouse. I think I understand what's going on, but just to be sure …. Perhaps afterwards we can retire to the dining room, tuck in to that cold collation for luncheon you promised me and imbibe with a glass or two of whisky. And you can relate to me about the incident in the fireplace again."

"But, I don't see the connection to that either."

"Nevertheless ..."

We entered the manor grounds, and the brooding physic garden with the sundial, box hedges and the low, sandstone walls that enclosed it. The lingering scent of herbs within always calms me and helps me imagine the monks – the inhabitants during the manor's previous existence as a priory – toiling among the plots of soil. Next, we traversed the lawns with the topiaries of yews and the wood sculptures of nature and mythical beings that my Love – she, the love of my life – had so beautifully crafted. We moved on to the grassed causeway, which is flanked by ancient oak, elm and ash and forms the approach to the gatehouse; a stone edifice with towering iron gates that once formed part of the boundary walls of the priory. The winter sun had risen above the skirt of denuded trees, but still hung low in the wispy clouded sky. It lay dead ahead and its dazzling rays split through the boughs and branches and blinded us.

It was cold and I looked forward to the whisky – I don't know why Eckersley was leading us here, when the main sighting of the apparition was on the landing of the first floor. I thought of the white dress hanging on the wardrobe and cursed at my carelessness – it was inevitable that he would pick up on that; I should have hidden it away. And all the while Eckersley was nodding, concluding ... and yet not judging me. He was too great a friend; I took comfort in that.

But when I gazed around me, in spite of the drab and bleak colours of a winter's morning, the flowerbeds lying dormant and littered with seed, shone as bright as the sculptures scattered among the bushes and lawns. And I thought of my Love. None of this would have been possible – the rebirth and renewal of the grounds, and the gutting and renovation of the manor's interior – had it not been for her.

***

We sat at the end of the sprawling oak table amid the stone walls of the dining hall, and between the regiment of empty chairs flanking us. Eckersley surveyed the cold collation spread before him.

"It's all to do with the light and how it plays tricks," he said as he sipped his whisky and reached for another chicken leg. "Passing headlights from the road during the rush hour." He refrained from using the word 'elementary' in a vain attempt to spare my feelings. "They catch the white dress hanging on the wardrobe handle, then travel along the corridor at great speed, the beams bouncing off the glass panes of the display cabinets; a myriad of pulsing lights, which somehow vanish through the wall, an area still unaffected by the breaking day. A brief spectacle, a blink of an eye, and it's done with."

"But, I *told* you. She appears again moments later, down the path where we just walked, as if she's running and holding her skirts, and comes to rest by a small tree near the gatehouse. A lingering, glowing patch – golden, I'd say – then it snuffs out."

Then … when I gaze from the oriel, and to where the early morning shadows have replaced the spotlight of gold, I catch her – just for a moment, and out of the corner of my eye – and yet when I look full on, she's disappeared, and instead I see the bared tree, which blends with the others. So eerie, as though she's staring at the house … or at me. I stopped short of telling him that; he'd only say something like, "Oh, it's what you *want* to believe … that it's *her*."

He must have sensed my frustration, and changed his tone. "Still, now that I'm here, tell me what happened in this room. The early eighteen hundreds, you say?"

I sighed. "I first learned about it soon after I'd bought the place at auction and was deciding what to do with it. The whole interior needed gutting—"

"Yes, and that's another thing," he interrupted me. "The wainscotting, the panels, the dark wood crossbeams and even the corbels are all modern, reproduction, *fake*. Sorry, I've no wish to offend you, my oldest friend, but the same goes for the hallway and grand staircase. They are airy and filled with light and afford no place for spirits of the afterlife to dwell."

"But the shell – the stones and walls – are original, along with the artefacts in the display cabinets. Surely you would acknowledge that these components are full of the echoes of times past. They carry the imprints of history; of emotions and dramas that occurred within these rooms, both as a priory and its subsequent incarnation as a manor house after the Reformation. The stone tape theory? Look at the collection … ceramics, religious manuscripts and works of art, and an array of debris and masonry and work tools unearthed in the grounds from the time of the monks. We made sure – my Love and I – that we kept them. It meant so much to us."

He peered at me through his steel-framed spectacles, his eyes wide, and placed his glass on the table. "OK, I'll concede; now *what* occurred in this room?"

"A dinner party, two hundred years ago, in *this* hall. Perhaps a masked ball, dancing, a string ensemble, lords and their mistresses feasting and frolicking; whatever – you decide. A maid, barely eighteen years of age, on a mission, decides to climb inside the recess of the stone fireplace, mount the chimney stack and lie in wait. She perches on the sweepers' stepping-stones and crossbeams, intent on playing a prank on the incoming diners – the young lord and his hangers-on and cronies. Maybe her motive was to correct a wrong-doing and she planned to leap out and confront them … or merely to eavesdrop; no-one knows for certain, but she would not emerge alive. A grisly fate; perhaps she got stuck, or suffered a seizure of some kind, but it wasn't until the next day, when the coals of the fire burned fierce and bright and the smell of burning meat wafted through the hall and beyond, that her mortal remains – that is, the charred bones upon her melted flesh – were discovered.

"And – this, you'll appreciate why it has upset

me so – there was, according to witnesses, so the story goes, a creature clutching at the corpse: the skeleton of another … a grotesque, not human, with a skull like that of an infant, and grossly disproportionate to the diminutive size of its body; a goblin, an evil spirit with hooked eye-sockets and grinning, razor-sharp teeth protruding from its jaw. The tapering fingers of an extended arm were wrapped round the unfortunate girl's ribs, and the other limb, resembling the bones of a bat's wing, was gripping its talons at her throat, as though stifling her scream."

I ceased my narrative, self-conscious, and unsure of my friend's reaction. He stared at me, picked up his glass and sniffed. "An unborn foetus – a result of the unfortunate's dalliance with the lord or his acolytes."

"Well it freaked me out for a long time – to think it occurred in this very room. I hate the thought of malignant vibes suffusing the hall, tainting my Love's adoration of what was to be our home. Besides, I'd invested everything I had in this building renovation project; I couldn't just leave."

"Oh, forgive me, I don't mean to be so dismissive. I merely suggest that like all ghost stories, it has probably been embellished by each successive narrator throughout the generations. If as you say, your Love calmed you and helped you fulfil the dreams that inspired you both regarding the renovations, then all well and good, but I must also conclude this has nothing to do with what you think is manifesting on the landing. That, as I have explained, is a result of your grieving."

Eckersley's tell-tale nervous glance across his shoulder towards the now empty, grey stonework of the fireplace – save for the innocuous décor of dried grasses, brass and pewter bric-a-brac – prevented me from feeling upset over his cold, forensic conclusion. That peek spoke volumes; his dismissive resolve was a deception. Who was he trying to convince? Me or him?

He noticed me watching him – my silent reproach – and he stiffened. "So what became of their remains – the maid and the so-called evil spirit?"

"Of the creature, I've no idea. The maid was buried in an unmarked grave in the parish churchyard. Covered up, forgotten; such was the power of the nobility. Another whisky?"

***

We parted with goodwill the next day, my oldest friend and I. He looked at me with concern and clasped my shoulder. "Sorry I couldn't help you, old boy, but if you need me, please call."

No psychic investigation then. He didn't believe me.

After I'd watched his car disappear down the lane, I retraced our steps along the wooded pathway to the gatehouse. A damp mist hugged the air; it thickened with smoke pouring from a brazier of burning twigs and leaves, and its acrid smell filled my lungs. Graves, the gardener, was stoking the pyre with a fork. His stoop, greying beard and bedraggled woolhat made him appear as ancient and gnarled as the surrounding spinney.

I greeted him with a wave of my hand. "I expect this is the last of the jobs before spring."

"Nah, much more to do. Thought I'd clear the path ready for the new growth." He shovelled a pile of leaves into the brazier causing a flurry of crackles and sparks. "Make way …."

As I backed off I stumbled onto a bush behind me; it almost reached my height. It's odd how I'd not noticed it before, especially as it stood apart from the wall of trees. I swore it wasn't there when Eckersley accompanied me yesterday.

"Awkward bugger that one,"Graves said. "If I don't get rid it'll be in the way of vehicles, passers-by and that. It's gotta go."

He picked up his spade lying on the ground.

"No, wait!"

That was it – the shrub where the point of light nestled. That was what I could see from the oriel. "Couldn't you dig it up … move it, I mean?"

Graves glowered at me. "Why ever do you want to do that? It's only an ash sapling."

"You don't know that; it's hard to tell what with it being devoid of leaves."

"They're two a penny 'round here. Where's the sense in that? And look here …" He stooped with a grunt. "See the mould on the stem? It's diseased."

"Even so … perhaps move it to the lawns fronting the south wing of the manor? The summer sun will catch it."

He tutted, chewed his lip and lowered the blade, tracing the edge as to where he estimated the roots would stretch.. "Hmph, I s'pose …."

I stepped back, allowing the choking smoke to envelop me as I watched him. He sliced at the turf and sifted the soil with surprising dexterity, until the blade hit something with a resounding clang. He dropped the implement, crouched and reached in the hole with his arm.

"What is it? What's down there?"

"Come an' look."

It looked like an urn, earthenware, as grey as stone and caked in mud. Bell shaped, bulbous with an elongated, tapering neck, it stood upright in the ground and faced the old priory gates, as though guarding the perimeter.

I lifted it from its hidey-hole, rather too eagerly judging by Graves's disapproving expression. I was just grateful that he hadn't smashed it. "Leave it with me; I'll take it to the house and get it cleaned up. It might sit well in a display case. Please continue to save the tree."

As I began my retreat I could hear Graves call back to me. "It's a witch's bottle, that's what it is. Plenty of 'em found over the years, 'specially in yon village. Worthless; don't mean nothin'."

I sat by the oak table in the dining hall, a bowl of soap and water and a scrubbing brush sprawled in front of me. A bellarmine jug – from the later period, I reckoned – I'd seen them before. For all I knew there were others hiding among the rooms throughout the house. We hadn't got around to cataloguing the contents before she – my Love – was struck down with her illness, and then … and then ….

I couldn't bear to go in some of the rooms anymore. I often ponder at what we could have found, what we could have discovered … together.

As I scoured, the glazing began to show on the wetted surface, in spite of the pits and crevices stained by dirt and time. There were features and contours – I could feel them as I traced my fingers over the pot. I soaked it with a sponge, wiping away the filth, and held it to the light, tilting it this way and that.

I could determine its nature now. A broad girth depicting an exaggerated pot-belly and navel with flattened breasts above, and the neck tapering to a head with straggly hair, wide eyes and a gaping mouth. A crone, hideous … yes.

I could see why Graves recognised it as a witch's bottle. A vessel used as a countermeasure to a witch's curse, designed to cast the spell back onto the witch. To ward off evil spirits.

For sure, considering where it was buried at the gatehouse, guarding the land. A talisman to quell a curse placed on the monks and their priory for whatever reason. But Christians would surely not succumb to such ungodly superstitions. No, I remembered, this dated from much later. The Lords of the manor … ah, someone held a grudge against them. A domestic dispute, a legal matter, a squabble with the oppressed and impoverished village folk, something of that ilk. The maid?

To ward off evil spirits.

An evil spirit … wasn't that how the creature that clutched at the unfortunate serving wench in the fireplace was so described?

I lifted the bottle and studied it. It was heavy; it rattled. An object was contained therein – the votive offering to ward of the spell. *The evil.*

I picked away at the seal – I knew I shouldn't; it was wrong for all sorts of reasons – and the wax crumbled to powder. I tipped and shook it, until the contents spilled onto the table. I had to know.

An effigy: a stick of wood wrapped in sackcloth and pierced with brass pins; one, two, three … it turned to dust, the air consuming it; its defiance of time cancelled within seconds. What else? Clay, gravel, some kind of dried seed, and … bones?

A rodent maybe, or a bird? No – diminutive phalanxes still attached to their hand and wrist, with talons for nails.

I recoiled, fist to mouth, and rose from my chair, its scrape on the flagstoned floor harsh and jolting. So the tale was true. The Lord of the manor got scared, buried the girl, and interred the creature away from the house.

I'm not sure what happened next; I can't remember. I may have retired to bed; a kind of distemper overcame me, a result of the winter's early evening shadows creeping across the hall, hiding the light of the new, reverting the manor to stone and the old. But it was on that very night, that my Love returned to me. I don't know whether it was a dream, a vision, or just a passing memory; it doesn't matter, it was so profound.

We were walking through the south facing garden where the sun beat warm, and cast its welcome augur on the flowerbeds - a kaleidoscope of colours dancing in the breeze. It must have been our first spring together at the manor - spring, the time of rebirth and renewal. She found the love token as she dug out and replanted the flowerbeds - a George III sixpence dated 1816 and curled inwards from the edges so that it would fit round the ring finger of the left hand. A token crafted for young sweethearts who couldn't afford an engagement ring for their betrothal. What a beautiful thing for us to find. I've worn it round my neck ever since that day.

The vision, the dream, was a sign; I knew what I had to do. As soon as dawn broke, I placed the betrothal token in the bellarmine jug and reinterred it in the exact location where Graves had unearthed it. The power of my Love would see me safely delivered, and a new era of peace and calm would be bestowed on me and my home.

***

I planted the sapling that I'd rescued from the fire and smoke in the same spot where she found our love token - at the edge of the lawn by the flowerbeds where the sun always seems to shine.

It is, as I had hoped, a rowan tree, not ash, as

Graves had asserted.

A rowan tree. Bane of witches; diviner of the future. It will live for two hundred years, I'm certain of that. It will protect me from the curses and the evil spirits; its berries so scarlet, bright and fecund. Red is the colour of magic and for warding off evil, is it not?

I shall sow some of the berries in the nearby churchyard, the resting place of the poor, unfortunate maid, as is the custom. I don't take cuttings, not from rowan – that is taboo.

I nurture the tree through the passing seasons. I adore how the light of the new year catches on the silvery grey of the bark, so smooth and exquisite, and the way it illuminates the purple leaf buds – a sure sign that life is renewed and never dies. I feel the sun's warm breath on the spring blossom – clusters of creamy white spiked petals – and wait eagerly for the canopy of lush green, feathery leaves.

And when the berries appear, as they always do, I know I'm safe.

But best of all, when I gaze upon the splendour, I think of my Love. I am reminded of how she thought, in wonder, about our distant ancestors' beliefs, from as long ago as ten thousand years, that, rather than limit ourselves to the linear concept of our mortality – we're born, we live, we die – we believe that our spirits merely transform, and appear in a different guise. They reside in the landscape around us – the hills, the stones, the streams, lakes and rivers, and the woods and creatures of the forests. Our human form is but a passing phase. She described it as the process of fluidity. I take comfort in that.

Her spirit lives on through The rowan tree. She is reborn and is present beside me. It … *she* never ages (as I do) and she'll stay with me for as long as I want; without end. Each time I attempt to cut and prune and slice, I'm sure I hear her cry.

When the autumn comes I shall exhume the bellarmine jug again and take some of the berries, and a scattering of her spent, golden leaves and place them inside where the love token resides.

For comfort and protection.

I don't fear the winter, the coming of the dark and of death, for I know she'll never die and will return in the spring, life renewed.

She'll always be with me, her colours, her aura so bright and vibrant. A force of nature that she was … ***is***.

My beautiful, sweet rowan tree.